RUNNING FROM THE REAPER

March rode toward the foothills, his rifle across the saddle horn, his eyes scanning the forested terrain ahead of him.

A minute later the skin on his back crawled, instinct warning him what was coming.

Knowing he wasn't going to make it in time, he swung the buckskin around and started to bring up the Winchester.

He caught a fleeting glimpse of what was behind him before his world collapsed into darkness.

The Gravedigger . . . rifle to his shoulder . . . a puff of smoke . . . a noise like thunder . . .

March felt a club hit him just above the left ear. The Winchester spun from his hands, and the suddenly vertical hardpan rushed to meet him.

Damn, the lunatic can shoot.

That final thought before he plummeted into the abyss . . .

Ralph Compton

The Last
Manhunt

A Ralph Compton Novel
by Joseph A. West

A SIGNET BOOK

SIGNET
Published by New American Library, a division of
Penguin Group (USA) Inc., 375 Hudson Street,
New York, New York 10014, USA
Penguin Group (Canada), 90 Eglinton Avenue East, Suite 700, Toronto,
Ontario M4P 2Y3, Canada (a division of Pearson Penguin Canada Inc.)
Penguin Books Ltd., 80 Strand, London WC2R 0RL, England
Penguin Ireland, 25 St. Stephen's Green, Dublin 2,
Ireland (a division of Penguin Books Ltd.)
Penguin Group (Australia), 250 Camberwell Road, Camberwell, Victoria 3124,
Australia (a division of Pearson Australia Group Pty. Ltd.)
Penguin Books India Pvt. Ltd., 11 Community Centre, Panchsheel Park,
New Delhi - 110 017, India
Penguin Group (NZ), 67 Apollo Drive, Rosedale, North Shore 0632,
New Zealand (a division of Pearson New Zealand Ltd.)
Penguin Books (South Africa) (Pty.) Ltd., 24 Sturdee Avenue,
Rosebank, Johannesburg 2196, South Africa

Penguin Books Ltd., Registered Offices:
80 Strand, London WC2R 0RL, England

First published by Signet, an imprint of New American Library,
a division of Penguin Group (USA) Inc.

First Printing, March 2011
10   9   8   7   6   5   4   3   2   1

THE IMMORTAL COWBOY

This is respectfully dedicated to the "American Cowboy." His was the saga sparked by the turmoil that followed the Civil War, and the passing of more than a century has by no means diminished the flame.

True, the old days and the old ways are but treasured memories, and the old trails have grown dim with the ravages of time, but the spirit of the cowboy lives on.

In my travels—to Texas, Oklahoma, Kansas, Nebraska, Colorado, Wyoming, New Mexico, and Arizona—I always find something that reminds me of the Old West. While I am walking these plains and mountains for the first time, there is this feeling that a part of me is eternal, that I have known these old trails before. I believe it is the undying spirit of the frontier calling, me, through the mind's eye, to step back into time. What is the appeal of the Old West of the American frontier?

It has been epitomized by some as the dark and bloody period in American history. Its heroes—Crockett, Bowie, Hickok, Earp—have been reviled and criticized. Yet the Old West lives on, larger than life.

It has become a symbol of freedom, when there was always another mountain to climb and another river to cross; when a dispute between two men was settled not with expensive lawyers, but with fists, knives, or guns. Barbaric? Maybe. But some things never change. When the cowboy rode into the pages of American history, he left behind a legacy that lives within the hearts of us all.

—*Ralph Compton*

Chapter 1

"They say Mr. March killed fifty men."

"They say a lot of things." The rancher turned to the car window and stared into the burned-out remains of the day. "He only killed as many as he needed to kill."

Lester T. Booker eased his celluloid collar away from his neck, sweaty from heat and irritated by grit and soot from the locomotive's chimney.

"Have you seen him shoot?" he said.

"At what? Men or targets?"

"Both."

"I never saw him kill a man. Never saw him shoot either."

"Pity. I'm told he's a crack shot."

"Who told you that?"

"Well . . . my editor."

"Where? Back in New York?"

"Yes, but he's read all the dime novels."

"Your editor knows nothing."

The rancher turned from the window. In the gloom,

his eyes were ice blue. "My ten-year-old son can out-shoot Ransom March any day of the week," he said.

"I find that hard to believe."

"Your first time out west?"

"Yes."

"Then you don't know any better." The rancher's smile was genuine but wintry. "Young feller, out here when you call a man a liar to his face or behind his back, you should be ready to back your play."

"I didn't mean to imply—"

"Like I said, you don't know any better."

Booker's prominent Adam's apple bobbed as he swallowed hard. He picked his words. "So, Mr. March can't shoot?"

"He can shoot."

"But you just said he couldn't. Oh, I see. You mean he's not a crack shot?"

"No."

"But how—"

A gun suddenly appeared in the rancher's hand and the muzzle pushed into Booker's belly. "That's how. This close, a man doesn't need to be a crack shot."

Booker shrank back in his seat. "He . . . he killed all those men—"

"Yeah, just like this, when he was close enough to spit on them. Ransom March ain't what you'd call a retiring man." The rancher shoved his Colt back in his waistband. "So, you're writing a story about March for the newspaper?"

"Yes, for the *New York Chronicle*."

"Rance know you're coming?"

"We exchanged letters and he agreed to be interviewed about the old days if I came to Santa Fe."

"I hope for your sake he hasn't changed his mind."

"Why do you say that?"

"Because he don't suffer fools gladly, Archibald."

Booker stiffened and his mouth pruned in prim disapproval. "Sir, I am not a fool and my name isn't Archibald."

"No? I fer sure took ye for an Archibald. All right, then you're not a fool, but you're a pilgrim and March don't take kindly to them either."

"He's retired, and this is 1890 and the Wild West is gone. Surely he's over his prejudices by now."

"Maybe, but he's still a handful."

"In what way?"

"You'll find out, Archibald. You'll find out."

When the rancher turned to the darkened window again, he grinned.

Chapter 2

Booker stood on the dark, windswept platform, a guttering oil lamp above his head casting shifting light on the top of his plug hat and the shoulders of his broadcloth coat.

"You waiting for somebody, young feller?" the stationmaster asked. He held a lantern that pooled around his feet like spilled orange paint.

"Yes. Mr. Ransom March. He said he'd meet me here."

"He'll be here, unless he pulled a cork. If he did, you'll see him tomorrow or next week."

"I'll wait."

"Suit yourself."

The railroad man walked away, then stopped and turned. "Coffee, what's left of it, in the waiting room if you'd care for some."

"Thank you, yes."

"He'p yourself."

The coffee was strong, black, and bitter, and it took the edge off Booker's tiredness. It had been a long trip from New York.

He stepped to the window and looked out at the deserted platform.

White moths fluttered around the oil lamps until they were blown away like snowflakes in the gusting wind. Coyotes yipped, hunting close, and from somewhere in town, a saloon piano tinkled notes, fragile as glass, into the darkness.

Booker closed his eyes and in a croaky whisper sang along with the tune that was then all the rage in New York.

After the ball is over, after the break of morn,
After the dancers' leaving, after the stars are gone,
Many a heart is aching, if you could read them all,
Many the hopes that have vanished after the ball.

"I've heard that sung prettier, but you'll do."

Booker turned and saw a short, stocky man grinning at him.

"I'm not much of a singer, I'm afraid," he said.

"Already figured that out for my own self."

"Did Mr. March send you?"

"No, he came in person."

"Is he outside?"

"No, he's right here."

"You're Ransom March?"

"As ever was." Booker's disappointment showed, because March said, "Who did you expect? Wild Bill Hickok maybe?"

Booker was too discouraged to make up a polite lie. "Yes, something like that."

March shook his head. "Bill was a pain in the ass, especially later when his nerves were shot and the French pox done for his eyes."

"You knew him?"

"Got drunk with him a few times." March looked the younger man over from the toes of his elastic-sided boots to the top of his hat. "You must be Mr. Booker."

"Lester T. Booker of the *New York Chronicle*, at your service."

March held out his hand. "Pleased to meet you."

Booker took the proffered hand and felt steel in the man's grip. He was relieved when March let go and he could flex his crumpled fingers.

"Funny thing, when I first walked in an' saw you, I took you fer an Archibald," March said.

"What does an Archibald look like?" Booker asked, his face stiff.

"Like you. Tall, skinny, no shoulders and chest, and no chin to speak of." March smiled. "That's what an Archibald looks like."

"The name is Lester."

"And Lester it is." March's blue eyes trapped humor like points of light. "Do you tell jokes, Lester?"

"No."

"Pity. I could have called you Lester the Jester."

"I prefer just plain Lester."

"All right, plain Lester, I have a buckboard outside. We can head for my place. I'll take your bag."

"I can manage it," Booker said.

Swallowing the dry ashes of his disappointment, he

picked up his valise and told himself that nothing about this assignment boded well.

He'd expected a very different Ransom March.

In his mind's eye he'd pictured a frontier cavalier in beaded buckskins, a prince of pistoleros standing more than six feet tall in handmade boots, his trusty ivory-handled Colts always at the ready to defend the poor, the weak, and fair, but vulnerable, American womanhood.

Booker had imagined a gallant who, when he cut a dash, made every female heart flutter as they breathlessly beheld his flowing hair and heroic mustache.

A paladin adored by women, envied and admired by men. That was the Ransom March Booker had expected.

Instead, in front of him in the gloom, walked a short, slightly bowlegged, thickset man, wearing a wool vest faded by sun into a pale orange color, frayed pants tucked into mule-eared boots, a shapeless, battered hat jammed far down on his gray head.

Booker's fantasy March had borne the handsome, noble countenance of, say, Hickok or the gallant Custer, but the harsh reality was that the old gunfighter bore resemblance to neither.

Ransom March was a plain, brown-faced man, badly in need of a shave, his huge handlebar mustache fringing a thin, tight mouth. His eyes were faded, used up, as though the sights they'd seen in his fifty-three years of hard living had worn them away.

He looked older than he was, slightly bent, his arms

corded with thick blue veins, his hands mottled, the fingernails like scaly horns.

In the eyes of twenty-three-year-old Booker, March looked exactly like what he was: a tired old man with all his glory days behind him.

The young reporter stared hard at March's back. For this he'd traveled all the way from New York . . . to interview the burned-out husk of a man.

Chapter 3

"Toss your bag in the back, then climb up, Lester."

Booker did as March told him, gingerly pushing away a shotgun lying on the buckboard's seat.

"It won't go off by itself," March said, grinning, placing the gun between his thighs.

He slapped the reins and then swung the team away from the station, rolling under a sky that flashed heat lightning from horizon to horizon.

It had cost Booker's paper a considerable sum to have him ride the cushions from New York to Santa Fe, and he decided he was duty-bound to try.

"Is that the shotgun you carried during all your Western adventures?" he asked.

March shook his head. "Nah, this here is a five-shot, Winchester model of 1887. It came too late for me."

The man held the reins in his left hand and built a cigarette with his right. He took time to light it before he spoke again.

"Had me a ten-gauge Greener, but I traded her a couple of years ago fer a bushel of green apples and three jugs of whiskey." March nodded, as though to himself. "Good gun, the Greener. Cut the barrels down to twenty inches and she handles just fine."

"Did you kill any outlaws with it?"

"Now, what kind of damn fool question is that?"

"They say you killed fifty men."

"With the Greener?"

"No, in general."

March looked at the sky. His nose had been broken and it lay flat against his face and it whistled softly when he breathed. "I don't know how many men I've killed. I've never counted them."

"Can I say you killed fifty?"

"Say whatever the hell you want."

"There was El Paso Pete Pinder. Remember him?" Booker had his pencil poised, notebook open on his knee.

"What about him?"

"He was the fastest outlaw with a gun south of the Red."

March smiled. "Was he, now?"

"That's what the dime novels say."

"What else do they say?"

"They say Pinder called you for a son of a bitch, then drew down on you outside the Ysleta Mission church in El Paso. They say you outdrew him and scattered his brains all over the mission door." Booker thought for a moment, then said, "That was back in the spring of 'eighty-two."

"My, my, is that right?" March said. "Good ol' Pete Pinder. He was a heller and no mistake. Had a fine mother, though, a churchgoing woman who never touched chawin' tobacco or strong drink."

Thunder rumbled in the distance and the air stood still. The only sounds were the hoofbeats of the team and the creak of the wagon.

"We're headed north by the way," March said. "Then we'll swing due west toward Black Mesa. My place is near there."

He turned and looked at Booker. "Got me a hired man, a man by the name of Lafe Stringfellow. He helps around the place in exchange for his grub and a place to sleep. If he takes a pot at us with his Sharps, pay him no mind." March smiled. "He's of a nervous disposition and prone to shoot folks by mistake." March looked at Booker. "But he's a steady enough hand when he's sober and at one time he was an army scout and a wagon train guide an' he fit Apaches. Later on, he and ol' Geronimo were almost like kin." March nodded. "Yup, good man is ol' Lafe."

Getting shot at, by mistake or not, didn't set well with Booker. But he shoved it to the back of his mind. Pete Pinder was a named man, and March had out-drawn and killed him. He needed the outlaw as a peg for his story and now he pushed it.

"Was El Paso Pete Pinder as fast as you thought he'd be?"

"I don't know."

"You mean you don't remember?"

"I mean I don't know."

Booker was irritated. The old man wasn't making this easy for him.

March said, "I got the drop on him."

"So you were faster." Booker squinted against the darkness and his pencil scribbled.

"No, I mean, I got the drop on him."

The old gunfighter fell silent again, his nose whistling. Then he said,"Somebody told me he'd seen Pete walk into Katy Moore's cathouse off Pioneer Plaza. I snuck round the back where the cribs were, just in time to see him climb off a whore by the name of High Timber. That gal was more'n six foot long, when she lay on her back, an' she done that a lot. Hell, I don't ever recall seeing her upright."

Booker, growing desperate, said,"And that's when you called Pinder out, huh?"

"I told you I got the drop on him," March said. "You ain't paying attention, Lester."

"Sorry. Tell me what happened next, at the Ysleta Mission, I mean. Did Pinder run there? Maybe seeking sanctuary?"

"Hell, boy, there wasn't no mission. Pete was in the cathouse, standing on one leg, pulling on his pants, and the window was open. So I shoved my Colt atween the curtains and cut loose. Shot him in the back of the neck and broke his spine. The bullet came out Pete's throat, right through the Adam's apple." March thought for a moment, then said,"Well, High Timber was still in the sack, one of them tall brass bed things. Well, dang me if the bullet doesn't tear through ol' Pete, hit the bedstead, and go right into the back of High Timber's skull." He shook his head. "So your dime novels got the story all wrong. There wasn't no church, and the only brains that got scattered that night belonged to a six-foot-tall whore."

"You . . . you shot Pete Pinder in the back?" Booker said. He was horrified, his eyes round in the gloom.

"I told you, I had the drop on him. What else do you do when you got the drop on a man?"

"Didn't . . . weren't you charged with murder?"

"Hell no, but I'd played hob. I recollect that. Katy Moore demanded five hundred dollars compensation, said she set store by her dead whore, and the city had to pay. Then Pete's ma came to take her son's body home, only he'd been dead and buried for two weeks by then and nobody would dig him up. Besides, they'd plumb forgot where they planted him.

"She went home by herself and has been grieving from that day to this, so I'm told. Unless she's dead by now."

"But you shot a man in the back."

"I surely did. You don't take chances with fast men like Pete Pinder. You kill them any way you can."

"You were a lawman then?"

"Yeah. Deputy United States marshal at the time. Ol' Pete had a wanted dodger on him, offered a five-thousand reward, dead or alive. I never did get the money. Damned government said I'd killed him in the line of duty and never paid a cent."

Booker was stunned into silence. This . . . back-shooting savage was not the man he'd traveled nearly two thousand miles to interview.

He'd made a big mistake, and he saw no way of rectifying it.

Unless . . .

"I prefer the dime novel version of the Pinder fight," he said. "You mind if I rewrite that? Maybe add the bit about his grieving ma visiting her son's grave and you letting her cry on your shoulder."

"I never saw the woman. But I told you, Lester, write whatever the hell you like. I don't care."

March drove in silence for a few minutes, then said, "See that white boulder up ahead? It marks the cutoff to Black Mesa. Be home soon, and I could sure use a cup of coffee."

"You killed an innocent woman," Booker said, his voice hollow in the motionless darkness. "Doesn't that trouble you?"

"Why should it?"

"I mean, because she was an innocent bystander."

"Hell, High Timber wasn't innocent. In her day, she'd cut a few drovers and one time she emptied a .22 pepperbox into a whore by the name of Big Molly Kilcoyn. Now, Molly dressed out at around four hundred pounds, so she came to no harm from them little bullets. But then High Timber got her knife and did some cuttin', swore she was going to carve Molly's nose off. Nearly did, as I recollect."

March turned and looked at Booker. "High Timber took her chances when she decided to consort with Pete Pinder and other low persons. I don't lose any sleep over her. And there's my cabin. Be ready to duck if Lafe's pulled the cork on the whiskey jug."

Chapter 4

To Booker's relief, they were met at the cabin door by a tall, good-looking black man with graying hair who seemed sober enough. He held a rifle, the barrel resting on his shoulder.

When he saw March he smiled. "Coffee's on the bile, boss."

"Any grub, Lafe?"

"Got some stew left."

"That will do." March waved a hand. "This here is the newspaper feller I told you about. Name's—"

"Don't tell me." Lafe grinned. His teeth white in the gloom. "It's Archibald, right?"

"No," Booker said stiffly. "My name is Lester. Lester T. Booker of the *New York Chronicle*."

Lafe's smile slipped as disappointment emptied his face. "Hell, I sure had you pegged fer an Archibald."

"So did I," March said. "Sometimes a man doesn't get the name he deserves."

Anger in him, and a niggling desire to wound, Booker

said,"And no one should know that better than you, Mr. March."

When he thought on it later, Booker realized that he'd expected March to match his anger, perhaps snap at him like a terrier does a rat.

But the old gunfighter only smiled, not sadly but in resignation.

"You're a judgmental man, Lester," he said.

"I can only form my opinion on the evidence presented to me," Booker said.

"Hell, you even sound like a judge."

"Better get indoors, boss," Lafe said. "Getting cool out. Remember your rheumatisms."

March stepped inside the door and Booker made to follow, but Lafe barred his way with an arm as thick as an oak fence post.

"I don't like you," he said, low, so March wouldn't hear.

Booker's gaze searched out the black man's eyes in the gloom. "Why do you say that?"

"Because you don't show respect to Mr. March, a better man than you'll ever be."

"He'll have to prove that."

"Mister, he don't have to prove anything to you."

"Lafe, don't detain our guest," March called out from inside.

"Coming, boss." Lafe grabbed a handful of Booker's high-button suit coat. "Mind your manners around the boss, Mr. Booker. If'n you don't, it could go badly for you."

*   *   *

Booker picked through his stew, eating the onions, potato, and carrot. The meat he left strictly alone.

"Don't like beef, huh?" March said.

"I don't eat any animal flesh, except a little fish now and then."

"Well, I don't have any o' that."

The reporter drained his coffee. March had offered to lace it with whiskey, but Booker didn't drink either. He laid his notebook in front of him on the kitchen table.

"When you were called in to tame a wild cow town, did you wear a special costume?" he asked. "Perhaps dressed all in black?"

"Black, brown, blue, gray, yellow . . . whatever I could get."

"Get where?"

"At the mercantile."

"For example, did you wear a frock coat?"

"Nah. Never could afford fancy broadcloth on a lawman's wages."

Booker felt as though he were hitting his head against a brick wall, but he persisted. "You spent money on your gun belts, though, decorated them with silver studs and the like."

"You mean a cartridge belt and scabbard?"

"Yes, exactly."

"Never had one o' them."

"How did you carry your gun?"

"Stuck it in my waistband or in a pocket."

Booker seemed to intently study the back of his hand, but in reality he was fighting down a feeling of hopelessness not unmixed with despair.

"What kind of guns did you use, Mr. March?"

"The kind that shoot bullets, Mr. Booker."

Lafe Stringfellow laughed.

"I mean, a rifle? A Colt?"

"Had me a .44-40 Winchester, model of 'seventy-three."

"Do you still have it?"

By way of an answer, March turned to Lafe. "Where's the rifle?"

"Under your bed, boss. Where it always is."

"And the Colt?" Booker prompted.

"It's around here somewheres," March said. "I had the barrel cut back to the same length as the ejector and the front sight made higher and thicker."

Booker smiled and scribbled. At least this was something, Ransom March, King of the Plains, talking about his Excalibur.

"Ivory handles, no doubt," he said.

"It's got rubber handles. That's how it came from the factory and I never saw a need to change them."

Lafe poured coffee for both men, not making eye contact with Booker. March held up the whiskey jug, his eyebrows raised, but the reporter shook his head.

"I promised my mother and my betrothed that my lips would ne'er touch strong drink, nor would I ever utter profanity or consort with fancy women."

"Is that a fact?" March said. Then, on a lower note, said, "Good for you."

He poured a generous dash of whiskey into his cup.

"Tell me about your most memorable gunfights," Booker said.

"Which ones?"

Booker's irritation was almost painful, like a nettle rash all over his body.

Any one, you damned, ignorant hick! Aloud he said, "Maybe a street fight you remember?"

"I never had a fight in the street. Oh, sure, I took pots at fleeing felons in the street, but never gun-fought nobody."

"A saloon fight, then?"

March thought for a while, then said,"I shot Jake Winter in the Alamo Saloon down McAllen way in Texas." He turned to Lafe, who was standing by the stove. "You recollect him, Lafe?"

"Uh-huh, boss. Wasn't Jake living with Saggy Maggie Whitley at the time? I recollect she had a simple son. What was his name? Benny? Billy? Something like that."

"Barney," March said after a moment's hesitation.

Lafe grinned and snapped his fingers. "Yeah, that was it, Barney. Last I heard he got hung in the Nations somewheres for being a nuisance to damn near everybody."

"Whatever became of Maggie?" March said.

Before Lafe could answer, Booker said quickly, "Was Jake Winter an outlaw?"

"Jake tried his hand at a lot of things: cowboy, lawman, storekeeper, railroad conductor. Then he got into the bank and train robbing profession and figgered he'd found his calling."

"You were trying to arrest him?"

"You could say that. How it come up, I had a John Doe warrant and I reckoned ol' Jake fit the bill just fine."

Booker scribbled, then said,"Was Winter fast on the draw?"

"Hell, he got his weapon out quick enough that night, like a rube in a San Francisco whorehouse."

"What happened? Tell me every detail."

"Not much to tell. I said to Jake, 'I'm arresting you fer holding up the Katy Flyer, stealing a Wells Fargo strongbox, and killin' a shotgun guard.' Well, Jake took exception to that and called me fer a low person and damned scoundrel."

"Then he drew down on you?"

"Oh yeah, he skinned his iron and got to his work."

Booker's pencil hovered over his notebook. "Then what happened?"

"Well, we traded shots and pretty soon all the saloon lamps blowed out, from the guns, like. I seen Jake step out of the smoke like a ghost, trying for a clear shot, and I walked up to him, real close. 'You're a dead man, Rance,' Jake says. 'I got ye now.' 'Oh, am I?' says I. 'Then you're a better man nor I thought you were.'

"Well, I shoved my gun into Jake's belly and he did the same to me. Jake shot first and his revolver misfired, just made a click. Mine didn't. I pumped two bullets into his gut, and as he fell, another into his damned fool head." March smiled. "Dead as mutton when he hit the floor, was ol' Jake."

A silence stretched; then Lafe said,"Boss, you didn't tell that right. It was a bank strongbox. Saggy Maggie always said it was full of foreign bank bonds and no cash."

"Yeah, you're probably right about that," March said,

nodding. "Now I recollect Jake saying he didn't make no profit from the Katy robbery so he shouldn't be arrested." He shook his head, looking at Booker. "Jake Winter had a good heart. I think he took up with low companions was all."

Booker was silent for long moments; then he said, "An interesting story, Mr. March, but that's not how it happened."

Chapter 5

March was taken aback. "So maybe you were there?"

"No, but I have an eyewitness account of one who was."

"Who might that be?"

"His name is James Peabody, and he wrote this. . . ." Booker searched inside his carpetbag and came up with a slim, paperback volume. "It's titled *Ransom March, Six-Gun Marshal*, and your fight with Jake Winter is mentioned. Shall I read it to you?"

"There wasn't a ranny named Peabody in the Alamo Saloon that night," Lafe said, thunder in his eyes.

"I beg to differ," Booker said. "It's all down here in black-and-white."

"Let Mr. Booker read it, Lafe," March said. "He seems to know more about the Alamo fight than we do."

Booker thumbed through the dime novel, the rippling pages making a *tick-tick-tick* sound.

"Ah, here it is," he said. He cleared his throat and read in a well-modulated, expressive voice:

CHAPTER SEVEN

Peril on the Plains, or The Maiden's Distress

It soon came to Marshal March's ears that the dangerous desperado Jake Winter was saying to all who would listen to his boasts in the Alamo Saloon that he would "shoot that damned lawman on sight." Worse, so much worse, he had accosted the local schoolteacher, pretty Miss Pamela Just, on the street and had dragged her, screaming, into his evil drinking den.

With a bloodcurdling curse, he told the swooning maiden that after he killed the marshal, he would take her to his room *and have his wicked way with her*.

"After lying with me, never thereafter will you desire another man," quoth that grinning braggart.

Upon his entering the saloon, the frantic girl made an impassioned plea to Marshal March, calling out in her dreadful despair, "Oh, kind sir, please rescue me from this vile ruffian, for I fear I'll be undone."

All present knew that a baker's dozen of victims had fallen to Winter's flaming Colts, but our six-gun stalwart, Marshal March, showed not the slightest sign of dread or apprehension. He then spake up like a true prairie hero.

"Fear not, fair lady, for I, Ransom March, have sworn a binding oath to protect *American woman-*

hood and to do all in my power to ensure that their maidenhoods are preserved intact until the day they enter that most sacred of all bonds, holy matrimony."

On hearing this fine speech, Jake Winter snarled another terrible oath and cried, "Marshal March, I intend to kill you on the moment, then despoil this fair flower and steal away from her that glittering crown she holds most precious, her chaste virtue."

"I will hear no more of this immoral, degenerate, and villainous talk," declared the valiant lawman. "Winter, you wear *a murderous revolver* at your waist, so produce it and get to your deadly work, for I, Ransom March, will not draw first on any man, no matter how foul a creature he may be."

"Then I've got ye now, Marshal," declared Winter as he, grinning like a demon, proceeded to draw his merciless weapon.

But ere anyone in that crowded den of iniquity had scarce time to blink, the Marshal's gun appeared in his hand as though by magic, and barked once.

Winter, his breast burst asunder by Marshal March's unerring ball, uttered a terrible cry, and then fell to the ground. "Oh, I am slain," he said.

"Yes, you have fallen to the forces of righteousness and law and order that must always prevail when the weak and frail are threatened by the legions of darkness," Marshal March said.

Miss Just, swooning once again, but this time

not from fear, but on beholding the Marshal's *brave and manly countenance* ran into his arms and declared, "Oh, Mr. March, you are my hero. Would that you might make me your virginal bride."

"Alas, fair maiden," quoth that Prince of the Plains, "I cannot yet settle down to such a blissful state, for I must continue to ride forth, righting wrongs wherever I find them."

He kissed Miss Just most tenderly, then took his leave of her, riding into the setting sun, his noble work, for now at least, done.

After he finished reading, Booker's words dropped like rocks into the pool of silence. "That's the story I want, only better," he said. "I'll play up a rogue lawman angle, add some details to the train robbery, and elaborate on the maiden in distress."

March and Lafe seemed stunned. Finally March said, "That's how it happened?"

"It's all here in the novel. Didn't you read it?"

"No, I reckon not. Don't plan to either."

March looked at Lafe. "Saggy Maggie was the only woman in the Alamo that night. Do you recollect another?"

The black man shook his head. "No, boss, only Maggie, and she wasn't no virginal bride. Her brothers had bust her cherry a long time before that night."

Booker's smile was smug, vaguely superior, a thing March ignored or did not see, but it enraged Lafe.

"They say big ol' Maggie could take on two punchers at one go," March said.

"Heard that," Lafe said. "But I don't believe it myself."

"Well, that's what they say."

"Saggy Maggie notwithstanding, I plan to make you a hero in spite of yourself, Mr. March," he said.

"Back east?" Lafe said. "Nobody knows the boss in New York."

"Ah, but they will. Newspaper stories back east worked for Wild Bill Hickok and they will work for Mr. March. His is a singular tale and of great moment."

"You don't have to make the boss a hero," Lafe said. "He is a hero."

"Yes, possibly, but not the kind that sells newspapers."

"Write what you want, Lester," March said. Suddenly he looked tired and old. "I don't care."

Booker smiled again. "Don't you worry, Mr. March. When I'm done with you, you'll come out smelling like a rose. I can make a silk purse out of any pig's ear."

March rose to his feet. "I've never smelled a rose. Have you, Lafe?"

"No, boss. But I'm sure smelling a skunk."

Chapter 6

Booker slept that night in an old bunkhouse that hadn't been lived in for years and smelled of pack rats and dust.

March and Lafe had done their best to make him comfortable, but his narrow iron bed squealed with even the slightest movement and the corn shuck mattress was lumpy and hard.

But, despite his discomfort, Booker felt better about his assignment.

He would borrow freely from dime novels about March and others, embellish the old gunfighter's exploits, and turn him into the Galahad of the Guadalupes, or something like that.

It seemed that March would not object to anything he said about him, and why should he? When Booker had arrived in Santa Fe, he'd found the old man a dull lump of coal, but his excellent prose would transform him into a diamond.

Well, a diamond in the rough perhaps, but nevertheless, a glittering masterpiece of the writer's craft.

Booker was smiling when he finally fell asleep, the coyotes calling out his lullaby.

"Breakfast in five minutes," Lafe yelled, shoving his head in the bunkhouse door. "And there're riders coming."

Groggy, his head aching, Booker said,"What manner of riders?"

"I guess we'll know that when they get here," Lafe said.

"Sorry I had to say it straight out, Rance. I didn't know how to cushion it. You see how it was with me?"

"I see how it was."

March had a question, but he did not address it to Sheriff Henry Quarles, a man he held in low esteem, but to the Paiute deputy who sat his pony next to him.

"How many, Ishom?"

"Four. Or maybe more."

"Where are they headed?"

"North. Aiming for the Colorado border, maybe."

"How long a start?"

"Two, three hours."

Now March looked at Quarles. "How bad was it?"

The sheriff's saddle creaked as he shifted his weight. "Their hired man found them."

"Henry, how bad was it?"

"Bad, Rance. Real bad."

March waited, his eyes cold on Quarles's face.

"Mrs. Brewster's feet were burned away." The lawman coughed. "They'd held them to the fire."

That cut March to the bone.

Martha Brewster had been so proud of her little feet, and when she was younger she could dance on them as light as a spring wind.

"And Matt?"

"Rance," Quarles said, "they were old friends of yours. You sure you want to hear this?"

"Tell me," March said, his face like stone.

"They made the old man sit and watch Mrs. Brewster being tortured. I guess they heard the story that he had money hidden away and used his wife to make him spill the beans."

"How did Matt die?"

"He was buried alive, and so was Mrs. Brewster. The cabin was ransacked, but all the hired man could tell was missing was a money box with a few dollars in it and Mrs. Brewster's silver locket and gold ring."

"Her wedding ring?"

"Yeah. Cut off her finger to get it."

March's eyes moved to the Paiute. "Ishom, can you tell me anything?"

"Four men, like I said. They rode shod horses and one of the mounts could be a gray."

"You found hair?"

"Yes. On a fence near the cabin. Found something else."

March waited. The Paiute would tell him in his own good time.

"The lightest man walked on a left leg made of a stick."

March's belly iced, like a man seeing the ghost of an old enemy. "The Gravedigger?"

"Maybe so."

"Hell," Quarles said, "the Gravedigger was hung by vigilantes up on the Picketwire years ago."

"His evil spirit returned from the grave and walks, maybe," Ishom said.

"Not on a peg leg, it don't," March said.

"Lots of one-legged men about," Quarles said. "The war seen to that."

"It could be the Gravedigger," March said. "You hear stories about men like him, some true, some not. But his home range was always close to the Picketwire."

"Rance, I'm going to telegraph every lawman along the line between here and the border and tell them to be on the lookout," Quarles said. "We'll hunt those animals down, depend on it. If it is the Gravedigger, we'll get him."

"Posse?"

Quarles shook his head. "You know the country north of here, Rance. Impossible for a posse. Besides, I'd never find men willing to stay out, maybe for weeks. After what happened, the married ones won't want to leave their wives, and after a few days, single men don't stick."

"Go out yourself, Henry. Find yourself some backbone."

The sheriff was taken aback. "That's a hell of thing for you to say to me, Rance."

"I'll ride with you."

"No, I'll work the wires like I said. It gives us a better chance of catching them four killers."

"Then I'll do it the old-fashioned way," March said. "I'm going to hunt them down myself and kill them."

"Rance, this is a job for younger men. There are youngsters wearing stars out there just itching to prove themselves against real live bandits."

"Be on your way, Henry," March said. "You've got work to do."

"Don't like me much, do you, Rance?"

"No, never have."

"Why? What have I ever done to you?"

"Nothing."

"Then why do you dislike me?"

"Because you're a hollow man, Henry. There's nothing inside that broadcloth you wear, no substance. You're a politician, not a lawman, and back in the old days, you wouldn't have lasted a week."

Quarles was offended and he let it show. "And you're a bitter man, hankering back to days that weren't nearly as good as you imagine they were. The best thing you can do for all concerned is to die and let the Old West die with you."

The sheriff swung his horse around, then said over his shoulder, "The old days aren't coming back, Rance. The sooner you accept that, the better."

Quarles rode away, but Ishom Potts still sat his pony. After a few moments he raised his hand. *"Viaje con Dios, mi amigo."*

March nodded. "And may God ride with you too, Ishom."

The man turned and rode into Quarles's dust cloud.

The morning was no longer newborn, but the sky to the east still showed scarlet, like bloodstains on blue tile.

Chapter 7

"Lafe!"

"Right here, boss, at your shoulder."

"Saddle my horse and pack grub for a week," March said.

"I'm coming with you," Lafe said.

"No, you're not. I need you to look after the place."

"My place is at your side."

"Count how many calves were dropped in the spring. And check the water hole north of the mesa. She will silt up by times."

"Boss—"

"Hell, Lafe, do as I say."

The black man looked hurt, but he said, "I'll sack up the grub."

"Lafe . . ." March searched for words, then, "I depend on you to keep this old place going."

"I'll see it to it, boss."

March, feeling like he'd just kicked a puppy, watched Lafe go.

"Interview's over, Lester," he said. "You better head back to New York."

Booker, who'd been standing in the yard in his long johns and plug hat, rubbed the chill out of his upper arms. "I'm coming with you."

"No, you're not. You'd slow me down."

"I can ride. Back east, I often ride to hounds."

"Can you shoot?"

A moment's hesitation; then Booker said,"No." Before March could say anything, he added, "I wouldn't miss this for the world, a chance to ride out on Ransom March's last manhunt."

"No. Hell, all you'd do is lie about it."

"Then make me proud of you."

"If I do well enough to make you brag on me, you won't print lies. Is that it?"

"Close enough."

"All right, you can ride along, if you can ride."

"I ride a great deal in Central Park."

"Sidesaddle?"

Booker refused to be baited. "No, Mr. March, English saddle."

"Seen one o' them oncet. Figgered it would be like riding no saddle at all." He waved to the corral. "Ask Lafe to put a noose on the paint mare. She'll work all week, race on Saturday, and pull the buggy to church on Sunday. We'll use the bay as a packhorse."

"What made you change your mind?"

"About what?"

"Taking me along."

March's smile frosted. "It suddenly dawned on me that I want to see you get your damn fool Yankee head blowed off."

Booker was mildly amused. "You're a one, Mr. March."

"Ain't I, though?"

The sun was still climbing as Booker and March rode away from the cabin at the brush-covered base of Black Mesa. The morning had turned hot and insects were already making their small music in the grass.

March turned his head and looked at Booker.

"I'm getting old, Lester, and that made me think about you."

Booker smiled. "I've aged you that much, Mr. March?"

"Call me Rance."

"Rance it is."

"No, Lester, I been feeling my age before you arrived. You ever think about death?"

"Can't say as I do, Rance, except maybe in abstract terms, what comes after, stuff like that."

"Well, I reckon when I turn up my toes, Lafe will wrap me in a blanket and lay me in the ground near the mesa. My nose and mouth will fill with dirt and slowly I'll molder away. Then, one day, a big wind will come up and scatter my dust across the plains, and no one will recollect that I ever lived."

Booker opened his mouth, but March waved him into silence. "A man wants to leave his mark, something to remind folks he was here. Some men chisel their name on a rock, others perform good deeds or climb high mountains, but they're doing the same thing, trying to scribble their name on history."

"Is that what you want to do, Rance? Scratch your name on history?"

"Yeah, something like that. I want people to know I was here and that I left the western lands a better place nor I found them."

March turned his eyes to the sky. "And that leads me to a question."

"For me?" Booker said, surprised.

"Yeah, for you."

"Ask away, Rance."

"What is a better legacy for Ransom March? The lies you tell, or how it really was? Is the perfume of a fair maiden in distress preferable to the sweat stink of a two-dollar whore at a Texas hog ranch? Is a man who says, 'Oh, I am slain,' then drops to the floor as I say a noble speech over him better than the image of a young cowboy coughing up black blood on a sawdust floor after I cut him in half with a shotgun? Do people need to know that the youngster died hard, cursing me, cursing his God, and cursing the mother who bore him?"

March looked at Booker again. "Tell me, Lester, which Ransom March would be remembered longer? The truthful me or the damned liar me?"

For a long while Booker rode in silence, trapped by the vast, forested mountains rising on all sides of the Taos Valley. There was no breeze and he was sweating, his celluloid collar chafing him.

Finally he said, "Rance, history isn't written in stone.

It's adaptable. All men like me do is take the facts and adapt them to suit the current public taste."

"And I don't suit the current public taste?"

"No. You're too rough, too . . . uncivilized." Booker smiled. "But I will adapt you for the better, Rance, depend on it."

"So, in other words I'll be remembered for a damned liar?"

"What is truth, Rance? That too can be adapted. What I write is still the truth, just a different truth."

March smiled. "Lester, just listening to you gives me a headache."

"It's not me that's giving you a headache, Rance. It's this damned heat."

"Adapt the weather, Lester. Make it cooler," March said.

Chapter 8

March led the way north, keeping the Rio Grande in sight as he and Booker rode across the rough, broken country between the Tusas Mountains to the west and the eastern slopes of the Sangre De Cristo.

"From time to time me and Lafe do some gold prospecting in the Tusas," March said.

Hot and uncomfortable, Booker was only vaguely interested. "Find much?"

"Some color. Enough to buy tobacco and a jug of whiskey."

"Are we going to take a rest soon?" Booker said.

"Getting tired, Lester?"

"I could use a cup of coffee."

"Time enough for coffee when it gets on to dark. Them boys are only a few hours ahead of us. We could come up on them soon."

The sun was making an anvil of Booker's head and dark half-moons of sweat stained the armpits of his suit coat. Under his trimmed mustache his lips were white with discomfort and his hips ached.

Beside him, March looked cool and as rugged, enduring and ageless as the mountains around them.

"Damn it, don't you ever get tired?" Booker said. He felt petty and mean and irritated.

March smiled. "Sure. I like my blankets at night, same as anybody."

"Don't you want to sit in the shade and drink coffee?"

"Yeah, I do. But when I'm hunting men, wanting ain't having."

For a few minutes they rode in silence, the only sounds the creak of saddle leather and the soft footfalls of the horses. Once a covey of quail burst out of the brush ahead of them, followed by a jackrabbit that bounded through the brush like a rubber ball.

"Tell me about this man you call the Gravedigger," Booker said finally.

March built a cigarette and took time to light it before he spoke.

"He was an undertaker once and it gave him a taste for burying folks. Only now he plants them when they're still alive."

"Why does he do such a terrible thing?"

"He enjoys it."

"That's all he does? I mean just go around and bury people?"

"No, he robs, rapes, murders, whatever takes his fancy, but most times it ends in a burying."

Booker's hand went to his skinny throat. "God, I'd hate to be buried alive."

"Uh-huh, especially in a box. When he has time, the

Gravedigger puts his victims in a pine box, says they last longer that way. He likes to dig 'em up too. After a few days, sometimes weeks."

"For goodness' sake. Why?"

"Well, some say it's to see how they struggled. The fear on their faces as they gasped for their last breath."

Booker swallowed hard. "Rance, did you bring an extra gun?"

March grinned. "Thought you'd never ask. He reached back into his saddlebags and brought out a nickel-plated revolver that he passed to the younger man.

"Lester, that's a Smith and Wesson .38 caliber pocket revolver, model of 1880. She'll hit what you point it at, including the Gravedigger."

"The Gravedigger—even his damned name scares me."

"Slip that revolver in your pocket and you'll sleep easier o' nights," March said. He looked at Booker and smiled. "Ever shot a gun before?"

"Never felt the need before."

"Well then, you've already learned the first rule of gunfighting."

"What's that?"

"Have a gun."

Booker said, "You never let any man scare you, Rance, do you?"

"Yeah, I've been scared. Usually by men like you."

"Like me?"

"Yeah, Lester, the most dangerous animal on earth is a coward with a gun."

Booker realized that March had not made that statement to wound. He had merely stated fact as he saw it.

The reporter felt his face flush and he almost snapped that he was not a coward. But he remained silent, knowing how lame that would sound.

Besides, March was right. He was afraid of the Gravedigger, of catching up with him, so what the man said must be true: He was a coward with a gun.

By midafternoon March drew rein a mile south of the nine-thousand-foot peak of Cerro Montoso that climbed above the piñon and juniper hills.

"There's a cantina and general store at the base of the mountain where you can get coffee and grub if you've a mind, Lester," he said.

"Sounds good to me," Booker said. He was surly, still smarting from March's coward remark.

"The place is owned by a gal by the name of Tiller," March said. "Maybe the Gravedigger and his bunch passed her way." March's far-seeing gaze went to the mountain. "Damn it all, Lester, the Gravedigger is close. I can smell him."

Booker felt the dread again. "We don't even know if he was involved in the murder of your friends."

"How many peg-legged men bury folks alive for fun?" March said.

"Only one, I guess," Booker said after a while.

"Damn right," March said. "The Gravedigger is an original."

Chapter 9

"I swear, Rance, you never look any older, just more cantankerous and mean."

"And you, Bessie me darlin', look prettier every time I see you," March said. "A sight fer sore eyes, as they say."

"Rance, you were always full of it. Who's your friend?"

"His name's Lester. He's a newspaper reporter and he came all the way from New York to write lies about me."

Bessie smiled at Booker. "Write the truth. There's enough tell lies about him." She studied Booker more closely. "You know, I took ye fer an Archibald."

Booker decided the name thing would no longer irritate him. "So do a lot of people," he said.

The woman wiped the pine bar with a dirty rag. "What will it be, boys?"

"I'll have whatever you got that passes for whiskey," March said.

"And you?" Bessie asked Booker.

"Coffee, please."

"A nice-mannered young gent." Bessie's eyes slanted to the three men sitting at the dugout's only table. "More than I could say for some in here." She leaned across the bar and whispered to March, "I think they're hunting trouble, Rance."

The old lawman glanced at the three, before turning away again. "Hard cases all right. They ain't the Grave-digger's bunch, are they?"

"God bless us and save us, no, I don't think so. I hope I never see that devil again."

"He hasn't passed this way?"

Bessie hesitated, then said,"Not lately, no."

March read the woman's eyes, then said,"What aren't you telling me, Bessie?"

"Nothing, Rance, it's nothing. I'll get your whiskey."

"Damn you, Bessie, tell me. Yesterday early, the Grave-digger's bunch tortured and killed two friends of mine, an old couple who never harmed a soul in their entire lives. The Gravedigger buried them alive."

March's eyes had lost all their color and were as hard and gray as hammered iron, bleak caverns to a bleaker soul.

"Rance, please," the woman said, "please . . ."

"Miz Bessie, can I see them again, huh, can I?"

The speaker was a tall, gangly farm boy, towheaded, his long, eager face untouched by intelligence. He wore an old cap-and-ball revolver tucked into his waistband.

A bad mistake the way things turned out.

Bessie seemed relieved. She turned away from March and smiled. "Cost you another two bits, rube."

The boy grinned. His teeth were yellow, a couple

rimmed with black. "I got it, Miz Bessie, and a lot more besides."

"Then drop it in the jar," the woman said.

She quickly undid her buttons and pulled her shirt wide.

Booker's jaw dropped. Bessie's breasts were magnificent, huge and firm, the nipples as thick as a man's thumb, the areola pink and at least three inches across.

He swallowed hard as the woman buttoned up her shirt again.

The rube took thoughts from Booker's head and put them into words. "Miz Bessie, in all my born days, I never seen the like."

"Well, boy, keep putting your two bits in the titty jar and you'll see more of them."

The farm boy had boasted of having money, and that attracted the attention of the men at the table.

One of the three, dressed in the threadbare, faded finery of the down-on-his-luck gambler, called out to the boy, "You have a fine taste in women, young fellow. I said that very thing to my friends here when you walked in. I said, 'I can tell by the way he cuts a dash that there's a gentleman who appreciates the finer things of life.'"

Being called a fine gentleman pleased the boy, who looked no older than eighteen. "I like to see Miz Bessie's tits," he said.

"And so you should," the gambler said. "They are quite . . . ah, unique." He smiled under his thin mustache. "By the confident way you carry yourself, I also perceive that you are a gambling man."

Again the hick was flattered. His slack mouth stretched in a grin and he said, "I reckon I am." Now he boasted. "I know my way around a deck."

"I'm sure you do, sir. May we interest you in a game of chance for small stakes?"

"Sure thing."

"Of course, sir, that is only if your funds allow."

"Got me near a thousand dollars," the boy said. "Stole it from the old farmer who raised me from orphan boy to . . . gentleman. For ten years he never paid me a dime, so I figured I had it coming."

"Kid, you got it coming all right," March said under his breath.

Chapter 10

The three hard cases wanted the rube's money fast, so they opted for what crooked gamblers called a short-con—three walnut shells and a pea.

They let the boy win at first, drawing him in, and after a few minutes he was twenty dollars ahead. Pushed by flattery and comments on his "gambler's luck," he began to bet recklessly.

And started to lose . . .

"Trouble coming down," March said to Booker. "Stay out of it." To Bessie he said, "Get over here, woman. I don't want you hit by flying lead."

Booker was baffled, by March and by the shell game.

"What the hell's happening?" he said.

"Nothing yet. But the rube will get angry and draw down on them three. It's the last mistake he'll ever make."

"Aren't you going to stop it?"

March shrugged. "None of my concern, or yours. The rube's man-grown, big enough to take care of himself."

It happened just as March said it would.

After his roll was gone, the farm boy realized that the pea had constantly been palmed by the shabby gambler. He jumped to his feet, accused the man of cheating, and went for the old hog leg in his pants.

The muzzle didn't even clear his waistband before two shots slammed into his chest. The boy fell, blood starting in his mouth, hit the floor, groaned once, and died.

The gambler stood, a smoking Colt in his fist. "You all saw it," he said. "He drew down on me first."

"We saw it," March said.

"What did you see?"

"The kid drew down on you."

"It was self-defense," the gambler said.

"It was cold-blooded murder," Booker said, his face white.

"Don't mind my friend here," March said quickly. "He sees a thing—history being made, you might say—then adapts it to his own taste."

Booker opened his mouth to speak again, but March glared him into silence. "Talk like that again, Lester, and the killing in here could become general."

The gambler looked at Booker, thinking things through, his touchy gunman's pride riding him.

He had already taken March's measure and decided the old man would be no bargain. There was little profit to be made from a close-up gunfight against a tough old buzzard who would take a parcel of killing.

The Colt's triple-click was loud in the sudden quiet of the dugout as the gambler lowered the hammer.

"I just wanted to get things straight," he said, shoving the revolver into his shoulder holster.

"Straight as a string, the way they turned out," March said. He looked at the dead boy on the floor. "Better get rid of that."

"We're leaving," the gambler said. "We'll drop him off somewheres."

"Make sure it's well away from here," Bessie said. "Dead rubes lying around will give the place a bad name."

After the three men left, carrying the dead youth, March motioned with his glass. "Fill 'er again, Bessie. And Lester here looks like he can use more coffee."

After they'd been served, March said, "Now, Bessie, tell me what you know."

"Rance," she said, "let it pass. More killing isn't going to solve anything."

"I'll judge that. Was the Gravedigger here?"

"No."

March took time to build a cigarette. He thumbed a match into flame, lit his smoke, and said behind a blue cloud, "Who was here, Bessie?"

"Rance, I honestly don't remember."

March looked around him. "You make a good living from this saloon and the store, huh?"

"I survive."

A rope strung across the end of the saloon separated it from the general store and Bessie's living quarters. His spurs chiming, March walked to the rope, stepped over, and glanced at the store shelves. He found what he was looking for: a can of coal oil.

March unscrewed the stopper and poured oil on the floor, then scattered more behind the counter.

"Wait! Stop!" Bessie yelled. "What the hell are you doing?"

"I'm going to burn this place down around your ears, Bessie." March thumbed a match alight.

The woman's face signaled her alarm. "All right, all right," she said. "Put out the damned match."

March blew the flame into a tendril of smoke. "Let me hear it, Bessie."

"Alvara Gomez came to the store just before noon for supplies. She said her son was back and we joked that a boy his age can eat his weight in groceries."

March's empty expression told her he was drawing a blank.

"Yeah, and so?" he said.

"Alvara has a cabin near the river, a couple of miles south of here on the west bank of the gorge. She's always kept an open house for men on the scout. But she says now that her son, Cordero, is home, she's going straight. She plans to set the boy up as a blacksmith and farrier. He was always good with his hands."

March smiled. "A touching tale of motherly love, Bessie, but why tell it to me?"

"Rance, I'm telling you because you'd probably find out anyway." The woman took a breath, as though gathering her courage. "Cordero rode with the Gravedigger."

"When?"

"I don't know. Before."

"Before what?"

"Before what happened to the old couple you told me about."

"How do you know?"

"His mother said he rode in this morning on a lathered horse. Cordero said the Gravedigger was crazy mad, talking about raising folks from the dead, and that he wanted nothing more to do with him."

March's voice tolled like a death knell. "Was he there? Was he at the Brewster farm?"

"I don't know."

"I swear, Bessie, I'll burn this place and you with it."

"You won't harm him, Rance? Cordero is a good boy and he's all his mother's got."

"Damn you, was he there? Was he at the Brewster place?"

"Alvara said he rode away when they started to torture the old woman. He didn't stop until he reached his mother's cabin. She said he was so scared, he was trembling."

Hell burned in March's eyes. "He was there."

"Rance, we can arrest him and turn him over to the law," Booker said.

"I am the law," March said.

"You don't wear a star any longer," Bessie said. "And you stood back and let the farm boy get murdered."

"He wasn't murdered." March drained his glass and thumped it on the counter. "He had an even break."

"He was a rube!" Bessie said. "And he was up against a professional gunfighter. You call that an even break? I call it murder."

"Call it what you want. It was none of my concern." March looked at Booker. "Ready to ride?"

"We don't need another dead boy today," Booker said.

"Are you coming or not?" March said.

"I'll ride along. Maybe this time I can save a life."

"And maybe this time you'll get yourself shot," March said.

Chapter 11

As they rode away from the cabin, Bessie stepped outside and yelled after them, "You dirty son of a bitch, Rance. Leave that poor Mexican boy alone!"

Booker glanced at March. The man's face looked like it had been carved from a block of mahogany.

"I think she's talking to you," Booker said.

"I know."

"She called you a dirty son of a bitch."

"I know."

"I wonder why."

"She's trying to protect Cordero Gomez."

"Oh, that's why. I figured it was because either you are a dirty son of a bitch or she's just mad because you didn't pay two bits to see her."

March was quiet for a while; then he turned and looked at Booker.

"Lester," he said, "keep up the son-of-a-bitch thing and I'll be very surprised if we get through another hour without me gunning you."

Booker grinned. "Now, gunning their ace reporter wouldn't look very good to the *New York Chronicle*."

"Go to hell," March said. "You and the *New York Chronicle*."

They rode south under a bruised sky that promised a summer thunderstorm, keeping the basalt cliffs of the Rio Grande gorge in sight. Now and then, through breaks in the rocks, Booker saw the piñon and juniper of the tableland give way to Douglas fir and blue spruce closer to the river.

A rising wind announced the coming storm, and lightning flashed in the clouds. Scattered raindrops ticked around the riders, kicking up Vs of dust.

March reached behind him, then buttoned into his slicker.

"I asked Lafe to pack one for you, Lester," he said. "There it is, jammed under your blanket roll."

By the time Booker had donned the slicker, the rain began in earnest and thunder kicked up over the Taos Mountains to the north.

"Should be coming up on the Gomez cabin soon," March said.

Booker scanned the rain-lashed distance in front of him but saw nothing but sagebrush and forlorn stands of piñon.

"Over there," March said suddenly, pointing to his left. "There's a cabin backed up to a rock face. Got some cottonwoods around it."

Booker didn't have the older man's long-seeing eyes, but as they rode closer he made out a small cabin, a corral, and a few outbuildings.

"No smoke," Booker said.

"Yeah. Strange, that."

March slid the Winchester out from under his left knee.

"Get behind me, Lester. The Gomez kid could be laying for us and that means gun work."

Booker sat his horse. "I don't think so. Look over there at the cottonwood by the corral."

March turned his head, rain cascading from the brim of his hat. He peered into the distance, then said, "Shit!"

He kneed his horse forward and swung out of the saddle. He walked to the cottonwood and jerked the shovel out of the ground.

"Two graves," he said as Booker joined him.

"Were they buried alive?" Booker said.

"I'd bet the farm on it."

"But . . . I mean, why?"

"No one runs out on the Gravedigger. That's why."

"Rance, they might not be dead yet. Those graves are fresh."

"Yeah, he took time to bury these two, and that means he's just ahead of us, maybe only fifteen or twenty minutes." March turned away from the cottonwood. "Saddle up."

"No! Damn it, they might be alive."

"They're dead, and the kid was going to be dead anyway. Let's go."

"We're digging them up, Rance."

Booker's hand was under his slicker. His fingers closed on the checkered butt of the Smith & Wesson in his coat pocket.

March's teeth gritted, his eyes angry. "Lester, I told you to get on your damned horse."

"The hell with you. Go after the Gravedigger by yourself. I'm bringing them up."

"Let them be, I said. If Cordero Gomez is still alive, I'd have to shoot him anyway."

Booker drew from his pocket and the .38 pointed at March's belly.

"Get digging, Rance, or I swear I'll pull the trigger."

March smiled. "I never argue with a man who's got the drop on me."

He turned toward the nearest grave.

Booker never saw it coming.

March swung around, fast as a striking snake. The iron blade of the shovel slammed into Booker's gun hand and he cried out in pain as the revolver spun away from him.

March dropped the shovel, stepped close to Booker, and drove a right hand into his belly. The reporter let out a gasp of pain, doubled over—and his chin met a hard left cross that sounded like a club hitting a side of beef.

Booker went down on his knees, then stretched his length facedown in the mud. He was vaguely aware of March standing over him and he tried to move, but blackness took him and he knew no more.

He woke with mud in his mouth and the taste of blood in his throat.

Slowly, Booker became aware of a rhythmic *thud*,

thud, thud. He struggled to a kneeling position, waited until his vision cleared, and let his eyes follow the sound.

March was digging into one of the graves. The other was hidden by hills of mounded earth.

Booker had made no sound, but March, with the heightened instincts of the gunfighter, felt eyes on him.

He paused, leaning on the shovel.

"The kid is dead. Maybe half dead before he was put in the ground. I don't know."

"The woman?"

"I'm working on it." March's shovel bit into the dirt again.

Booker lifted his right hand to his aching jaw, then instantly regretted it as his bloody fingers punished him.

"Lester, get over here," March said.

Booker shuffled forward, his head spinning.

March dropped to a knee, looking into the grave.

"I think the woman is still alive," he said.

Chapter 12

"Help me get her out of there," March said.

"Are you sure she's alive?" Booker said.

"Hell no, I'm not sure. But I thought I saw her eyelids move."

Booker took a hold of the woman's naked arm and pulled. Still covered in dirt, she did not budge.

"Damn it, Lester, lift her head," March said. "I'll pull on her arms."

"I'm trying," Booker said. "It's difficult with a broken hand."

"Your hand ain't broken, Lester. Bruised is all."

"And I suppose my jaw isn't broken?"

"I gave you a love tap, so that ain't broke either. Now lift her head, damn you."

Alvara Gomez was not a small woman, and it took a few minutes for Booker and March to lift her free of the grave's clinging soil.

"Her mouth's full of dirt," March said.

He hooked his finger in the woman's mouth and his

thick, horny fingernail scarped out dirt, pushing deep into her throat.

"I don't think she's breathing," Booker said.

March bent over and put his ear against the woman's chest.

"Hear anything?" Booker said.

March straightened. "Nah, but the rain is making too much racket. Let's get her inside." He lifted an eyebrow. "Hell, she must dress out at two fifty."

"She's dead, Rance." Booker shook his head. "I read once that a person buried alive can last about twenty minutes, tops."

"She may not have been under that long. I reckon the Gravedigger made her watch while they planted her son." March shrugged. "He's got a strange sense of humor that way."

He grabbed the woman's hands. "Now, when I give the word, lift her head and shoulders. . . ."

"She's breathing," Booker said.

March nodded. "Pour her some water from the jug over there, wash the dirt down."

Alvara choked on the water, but managed to swallow some.

"She'll come around in a few minutes," March said. "How's the jaw?"

"You damned near killed me," Booker said.

"Teach you to draw down on a man."

"This woman would've died if I hadn't."

"Thinking back on it, Lester, I don't blame you for

what you done. But I had to clock you, because you was getting . . . What is that big word that happens to women all the time?"

"I don't know. Angry?"

" 'Angry' ain't a big word, Lester. Wait. Let me study on it for a spell. . . ."

March snapped his fingers. "Hysterical. That's it. You was getting hysterical."

The woman laid out on her kitchen table groaned and tried to raise her head.

"She'll live, I reckon," March said.

"Yeah," Booker said, "and she's about to get hysterical."

March sighed as though Booker had placed a great weight on his shoulders.

"Listen up, Lester. It takes a man with a pair of balls to draw down on me. You did all right. You was wrong, but you did all right."

"Beware of a coward with a gun, Rance. You told me that."

"I know, but now I'm not so damned certain you're a coward. By and by, it's a thing I'll study on some."

Alvara Gomez suddenly sat upright and screamed, her black eyes wild.

"Easy, easy, gal," March said, stroking her hair. He could have been soothing a frightened horse or an injured puppy.

Alvara turned to him, remembered horror in her face. "Cordero!"

"He's dead, ma'am," March said. "And you came damned close."

The woman stared at him for long moments. Her face had drained of color and there were specks of dirt at the corners of her eyes and in her nose.

"They beat him," she said finally.

"I reckon so, ma'am," March said.

"Then buried him. My son was screaming as they threw the last shovels of soil on him. Mother of God, they made me watch."

"Was it the Gravedigger, ma'am?"

"He's a devil, a demon. Dressed in black for a funeral, a peg leg on him."

"How long ago, ma'am?" March said.

The woman shook her head. "I was buried, senor. There is no time in the grave."

March looked around the cabin. "Do you have whiskey, ma'am?"

"There is mescal."

"You need some, ma'am. Settle your nerves, like."

Alvara shook her head. "No. I'm going after the Gravedigger and I will kill him. My son's soul won't rest until I do."

"Leave that to me, ma'am," March said. "I plan to run him down and hang him."

"Then we will go our separate ways, senor." Alvara swung her tree trunk legs off the table. "But first I must get my son. I will not let him lie in unholy ground."

"We'll rebury him, Miz Gomez," Booker said, ignoring an irritated, slanting look from March.

The old lawman glanced out the cabin window where rain was washing away the last of the daylight.

"Be dark soon," he said.

"We have to rebury the kid, Rance," Booker said.

March bowed his head in thought, then said, "All right, we'll stay here tonight and pull out at daybreak." His eyes again went to the window, the panes running water like a widow's tears. "Damned tracks will be washed out by then."

"Rance," Booker said, "don't you think that they're washed out already?"

Chapter 13

They headed north, riding under dry, burnished gold clouds, as the sun shouldered above the Taos Mountains. The rain had stopped, but the air was thick and hard to breathe.

Ahead lay the brush flats of Sunshine Valley, then the soaring volcanic peaks of Ute Mountain.

The Gravedigger and his bunch were not far in front of him, March was sure of that.

Booker's right hand was bandaged and his jaw was sore and swollen. He felt that he'd tangled with a cougar and come out on the losing end, but March exhibited not the slightest concern or remorse.

Alvara rode a rawboned mule that the Gravedigger had not thought worth taking. The woman rode in silence, nursing her grief, her eyes red and swollen into pouched slits.

She carried a Winchester across the mule's withers, taken from under a floorboard in the cabin, another prize the outlaws had missed.

"How many do you estimate?" Booker asked.

"Six, I reckon," March said without hesitation.

"Do you think they know we're after them?"

"Maybe. The Gravedigger always ran with a breed by the name of English McGill, half Kiowa, half Irish, and all son of a bitch. If English is still with him, he knows we're here. There's another man, a gunman out of Valverde they call Fred Kelley, got his start in the Lincoln County War, riding with Bill Bonney an' that hard bunch. He's good with the iron, mighty quick on the draw and shoot."

March was silent for a few moments, then, "I fear those two just as much as I fear the Gravedigger."

Booker was stunned. "Rance, I thought you were afraid of nothing, no man who walks."

"You reckoned I'm like them brave boys in the dime novels, huh?"

"Well, yes, I did."

"Listen up, Lester. I've never been in a gunfight that didn't scare me, or called out an armed man who didn't give me an attack of the damned croup afterward when I studied on it."

"But . . . but you're Ransom March."

"Yeah, I'm Ransom March because no matter how scared I was, I kept on a-comin'. Man has to swallow his fear whole, an' it hurts like hell going down, like eating a porkypine." The old gunfighter smiled, building a cigarette. "That's how she goes, Lester."

Booker's prominent Adam's apple bobbed, and his eyes glazed like a fish on a hook. "Rance, suddenly I don't feel reassured," he said.

"And I hope you never do, boy. That's what will keep you alive."

"Senor March, riders coming," Alvara said.

March showed his irritation, throwing away his half-rolled cigarette. "See what you done, Lester, made me do all that talking so I took my eyes off the trail."

"Behind us," Alvara said. "Six men, riding fast."

March swung his horse around. Heat already lay heavy on the land, and the horsemen shimmered in the distance, their mounts and bodies strangely elongated.

"Damn, I can't make 'em out," March said. "Is it the Gravedigger?"

Alvara's eyes were good. "No, not the Gravedigger. Other men."

"Lester, fade some to my left," March said. "Keep your revolver handy, but don't show it until I tell you or you'll get perforated. Miz Gomez, get on my right."

The riders emerged from the rippling haze and shrank into armed men riding good horses. The Gravedigger was not one of them.

"Scared yet?" Booker smiled.

"Not yet, Lester. You'll know when."

"If any shooting starts?"

"That would be about the time."

But Booker did not expect trouble. All six of the men wore lawman's stars and they were led by a tall young man who seemed to be in charge.

"Howdy," March said. He sat relaxed on his horse, but his eyes were wary. "I reckon you boys are on the trail of the Gravedigger, same as us."

"Name's Sheriff Cass Logan," the young man said,

"out of Antonito, a town across the Colorado border."
He smiled, a reckless blue fire in his eyes. "Any of you
make a move toward a gun, I'll kill you."

March said nothing, sitting still in the saddle, but
Booker was shocked and outraged.

"Now, see here, my good man," he said. "My name
is Lester T. Booker and I'm a reporter for the *New York
Chronicle*. I do assure you that it would go badly for
you if—"

"You?" Logan looked at March.

"Name's Ransom March."

"Out of the Santa Fe country?"

"Around there."

"I've heard of you." His eyes shifted to Alvara. "She
your whore, March?" He nodded to Booker. "Or does
she belong to Archibald there?"

"I am no man's whore," the woman said, her eyes
boring into Logan's face. "Is it because you're a son of
a whore that you ask such a question?"

"You shut your trap, you fat bitch, or I'll take a
dog whip to you," Logan said, his eyes ugly.

March leaned forward in the saddle. "Hey, Stretch,
what did you say your name was?"

"Cass Logan. There are men who know it."

"Yeah, I'm sure there are." March spat. "A word of
warning—don't ever talk like that to a woman in my
presence again."

Logan looked around him at his men, enlisting his support for what he planned to say next. "You don't scare
me, March. You earned your reputation back-shooting
drunks and cowboys."

March nodded, his face unchanged. "And I'm calling you out for a damned liar."

Logan's grin was twisted, a mix of triumph and latent sadism. He swung out of the saddle, then looked up at March. "I'm going to drag you off that hoss and beat some respect into you."

March stayed where he was, letting Logan come to him.

He judged the timing of his kick perfectly.

Chapter 14

March's left leg shot out, straightened, and the heel of his boot slammed into Logan's upturned face.

Booker heard the dry twig snap of Logan's nose breaking; then the lawman staggered back, a lacy halo of blood erupting around his head.

But it ended there.

Five guns leveled at March, and Booker knew they were only a single intake of breath away from a gunfight. He felt the Smith & Wesson, heavy in his coat pocket, and drew no comfort from it.

"No!" Logan yelled. He sounded like there was a rusty clot in his throat. "I want them alive." He glared at March with eyes that were already swollen and black. "You old bastard, you broke my nose."

March nodded. "Yeah, sonny, meant to do that."

"You're all going to die, March," Logan said. Blood leaked down the front of his shirt. "I swear, you'll die slow, cursing God and the poxed whore that bore you."

March shook his head and made a *tut-tut-tut* sound with his tongue. "I never expected to hear that kind of talk from a man wearing a star," he said.

"You'll hear that, and worse, old man."

Logan's long-barreled Colt came up, smooth and fast.

"Hamp, take their guns," he said. "They're going to the mountain."

The man called Hamp was a huge, surly brute with a scar on his cheek from a knife that had destroyed his left eye, leaving it as white as a seashell. His vicious features were a match for his mind.

He took March's Colt and rifle, but Booker spread his coat wide. "I'm a writer," he said. "I don't carry weapons."

Two things stood in Booker's favor.

Logan, arrogant, and with his own ideas of what constituted manhood, had already dismissed Booker, tall, skinny, and chinless, as an Archibald and did not expect him to be armed.

The second was that the only danger—March's skill with a gun—had been neutralized now he'd been disarmed. The old cougar had been defanged and wasn't a threat to anyone.

Hamp Lane obviously felt the same way. He ignored Booker and asked, "What about the woman, Cass?"

Logan dabbed at his nose with the back of his hand, then studied the glistening blood. Without looking up, he said,"You want her?"

"Don't like 'em fat," Lane said, "especially a greaser bitch."

"Anybody else?"

Logan got some dirty talk, but no takers.

"Then kill her," he said.

Alvara was taken aback, and after a few moments tried to swing her rifle into play.

Hamp Lane didn't need that long.

The woman was till trying to level the Winchester as three of his bullets slammed into her body. Alvara yelled something in Spanish that Booker didn't understand and toppled off her mule in a flurry of white petticoats.

"You damned murderer!" Booker yelled, his eyes as round as marbles.

He dug his heels into his horse and charged at Lane.

The big man didn't seem to exert himself. He casually sidestepped the charging horse, raised his right arm, and yanked Booker out of the saddle, throwing him over his mount's rump.

Booker landed on his back, all the breath going out of him. He tried to rise, but ended up on all fours, gasping.

Lane's boot swung and thudded into Booker's face.

His world exploding in fire around him, Booker slumped onto his side, vaguely aware of Lane looming over him.

Then a voice from the end of tunnel. "Want me to finish him, Cass?"

"Hell no. Too quick. Let the mountain do it."

Booker again tried to get to his feet. From faraway he heard March say, "Let him be. He's had enough."

Then a boot slammed into his ribs and the ground opened, swallowed him whole, and he plummeted into a darkness streaked by rockets trailing sparks.

Chapter 15

"Damn it all, boy, I figgered you were a goner fer sure."

Booker's eyes fluttered open. March stared down at him, his face close.

"Where . . . where the hell?" Booker said.

"Near as I can figure, the ridge behind me is Big Costilla Peak, goes maybe close to thirteen hunnered feet above the flat. I reckon we're about six miles due east of Ute Mountain and it's coming on nightfall."

Booker tried to sit up, but March pushed him back.

"Easy, Lester. You took a beating, boy."

Booker tried to piece together what had happened to him, but his brain was fragmented, like broken glass, and he couldn't think straight.

"Why are we here?" he said finally.

It took March a moment. "Well, there are two ways of looking at that. Logan says he wants us to reduce the Costilla ridge to a heap of rubble with picks and sledge-hammers. Now, Hamp Lane says it straight out, that he plans on working us to death."

March smiled without humor. "Either way, our futures don't stack up to much."

Making a huge effort to get back on track mentally, Booker said,"Why?"

"Why what?"

"Damn it, Rance, why did Logan, a lawman, do this to us?"

March didn't reply at once. He looked around him into the gathering dusk. The first stars were awakening, blinking like fireflies, and behind his head the dark bulk of Costilla Peak soared like the ramparts of an ancient fortress. The sky was streaked with scarlet, gold, and fish scale gray, the colors of a medieval battlefield, and the air smelled of stone and pine.

Rance turned his eyes to Booker again.

"To answer your question: Back there"—he waved a hand to the north—"are the Culebra Mountains. In the old days, the plains Indians used to harvest lodgepole pine from the slopes, for their lodges, like."

March fell silent and Booker said,"Go on, I'm listening."

The old lawman moved and Booker heard the chime of iron.

"But there's something else back in them peaks," March said.

Another pause, and Booker, growing irritated as his head cleared, said,"Damn, Rance, why don't you just spit it out and I'll read it?"

As though he hadn't heard, March said,"They say the old Spanish padres hid a fortune in gold church vessels in them hills. A lot of men died trying to find the treasure, but so far none of them succeeded."

"What's that to do with you and me? Does Logan want us to chip away the whole mountain range until we find it?"

"He doesn't have to."

March moved his legs and again Booker heard the clank of metal.

"He knows where it is?" Booker asked.

"No, but the Gravedigger does. Or so they say."

"Who says?"

"Folks in the know." As though he realized how inadequate his answer was, March added, "Three, four years back, the Gravedigger led sixteen men into the Culebras, hunting for the treasure. He came back out, but none of the others did.

"Except one."

"Help me sit up, Rance," Booker said.

"Slowly, boy, or your head will spin."

Booker's head did spin, wildly. And it was only after it settled that he discovered his legs were shackled. He kicked at the thick chains, drawing a smile from March.

"It's no good, Lester. You're chained to me—and both of us are manacled to that."

Booker followed March's nod. A heavy iron padlock attached the shackles to a steel staple that was driven deep into the side of a massive, granite boulder.

Using his uninjured left hand, Booker yanked on the chain. Metal clanked on rock, but the staple didn't budge.

"Better lay off that, Lester," March said, "or you'll bring Hamp Lane down on us, and he ain't an agreeable man."

"You told me one of the Gravedigger's men survived," Booker said.

He peered into the darkness. As far as he could tell, he and March were imprisoned in a narrow, tree-lined valley. To his right, a lamp glowed orange in the side window of a small cabin, presumably their jailor's quarters. Behind was a corral and lean-to barn.

"What happened to him?"

"The story goes that he crawled out of the mountains more dead than alive," March said. "He told a wild tale about the Gravedigger finding the Spanish treasure, then blowing up the entrance to the cave, burying all his men alive."

March, frowned in thought, then said,"Now that I recollect, the man's name was Jake Miles or Miller, something like that. He said he'd been away from the camp when the Gravedigger did for the rest of the men. Well, the story is that Miles went back into the Culebras to bring out the gold and was never heard from again."

"You think Logan is in cahoots with the Gravedigger?"

"Could be. That's why he took such offense when I told him we were tracking him."

"Seems like a strange alliance, a lawman and a cold-blooded killer."

"Lester, you still haven't learned that they're often one and the same. Besides, if the Gravedigger promised Logan a share of the Spanish treasure"—he stared into the darkness—"well, a man might be willing to sell his soul for that."

"Would you?"

"I'd study on it, fer sure," March said, smiling.

Chapter 16

The moon rose higher in the lilac sky, then impaled itself on a pine, and the wind tried to shake it free. A pair of hunting coyotes called close, their cries echoing through the darkness.

The cabin door swung open and Hamp Lane stepped outside. He unbuttoned his pants and pissed against a tree before going back inside.

A few minutes later a rider drew rein outside the cabin and he and Lane had a brief conversation. Lane laughed, then waved a hand as the rider cantered away.

The big deputy stood still for a few minutes, looking in the direction of Booker and March. Then he entered the cabin again.

"Damn it," Booker said, "I can't swing a sledge-hammer. I think Lane broke a couple of my ribs."

"Maybe you won't have to," March said.

"How so?"

"You've got the Smith and Wesson."

"I can't shoot Lane." Booker was horrified. "Besides, I'd be sure to miss."

"Let him come close, then shove the gun into his belly and pull the trigger. Done."

"I'd look into his eyes and I'd see a human being with a young man's life in him." Booker shook his head. "I can't do it."

"Hell, Lester, back at the Gomez cabin you were willing enough to shoot me."

"I wouldn't have, though."

"Just trying to scare me, huh?"

"Yes. But you don't scare easily."

"Not as a general rule. Pass me the gun."

Booker did as he was told and March shoved the little revolver into his coat pocket.

"Now what?" Booker said.

"Now we wait and see."

But Ransom March had been retired for a couple of minutes too long.

He'd forgotten that Hamp Lane, an experienced and canny gunman, would take no chances with him.

When the cabin door opened and Lane walked toward them, he was carrying a sawn-off Greener. With a weapon like that, even a gut-shot man would have time to cut loose with both barrels.

Seeing the man come, March put the Smith & Wesson to the back of his mind. It was thin, but he'd wait and hope that Lane would let his guard down.

"Not much hope of that," Booker said.

"Huh?"

"Didn't you hear me? I said maybe Lane will bring us coffee. It's getting cold out here."

"Good news, boys," Hamp Lane said. He stopped in front of March. He'd been drinking, but the Greener balanced easy in his hands.

"What's your news, Lane?" March said.

"You don't have to swing a hammer, neither of you."

"How come?" March said.

"Because I was just told that a gentleman is coming here to take care of you personal, like."

"Logan?" Booker said. He sounded like he already knew he'd taken the wrong guess.

"Hell no. Sheriff Logan is a busy man. He doesn't waste his time on riffraff and low persons like you."

"Then it's got to be the Gravedigger," March said.

Lane grinned. "Give that man a cee-gar."

Neither Booker nor March spoke, but Lane talked into the silence, enjoying himself immensely.

"I reckon you boys will be laid to rest sometime tomorrow afternoon." Lane's eyes glittered in the moonlit gloom. "If you like, I'll put flowers on your grave."

"Lane," March said, "piss on you."

For some reason known only to himself, the deputy thought this was funny. "Damn it all, I like you boys," he said. "Tell you what, it's my birthday tomorrow, but since you'll only be around for part of the day, why don't we celebrate tonight?" Lane cradled the shotgun in his left arm and patted Booker on the head. "What do you say, Archibald?"

March answered for him. "What with, Lane? Cake and ice cream?"

The deputy shook his head. "I ain't got none o' that,

but I got me a jug o' gen-u-ine Clinch Mountain bust-head, and then another."

"All right, undo the chains and we'll celebrate in the cabin where it's warmer," March said.

Lane grinned and shook his head. "Won't go, old-timer. I'll bring the jug here. A few drinks to warm us up an' we'll be cozy as bedbugs."

Booker opened his mouth to speak, but March talked over him. "Sounds real good, Hamp. Let's have at it."

"Be right back," the deputy said. "Now, don't you boys go nowhere." He stepped away, then paused and looked at Booker. "Archibald, anybody ever tell you that you look like a plucked chicken? A right scrawny plucked chicken ready for the pot?"

"Did anybody ever tell you—" Booker began, anger thickening his voice.

"That we're thirsty here," March said quickly.

Lane was silent for a few moments; then his eyes turned menacing. "We don't want no disrespect for a sworn officer of the law, do we?"

"No disrespect intended, Hamp," March said. "Ain't that right, Mr. Booker?"

Booker caught March's drift and swallowed his irritation.

"I was just going to tell you that my name's Lester," he said.

Lane grinned, his good humor restored. "No, it ain't. It's Archibald. And you still look like a damned chicken wearing a plug hat."

As his gaze followed Lane back to the cabin, Booker said, "God, I hate that man."

"Fer callin' you Archibald?"

"That, and for what he did to Alvara."

"Well, you won't have to hate him much longer."

"How come?"

"Because I plan to kill him before sunup," March said.

Chapter 17

Hamp Lane passed the jug to March. "Drink up, old-timer. Next time you pull a cork, you'll be in hell."

March raised the jug. "Well, happy birthday, Hamp, and may you have many, many more."

He put the jug to his lips, but drank very little. Then he offered it to Booker.

"I don't want any," he said, holding up a hand.

"More for us, Rance, huh?" Lane said.

"Sure is, Hamp." March lifted the jug again, but this time he only pretended to drink. He passed the whiskey back to Lane.

An hour passed. The moon climbed higher in the sky and to the north dry lightning flickered. A desert chill rode on the wind, trailing the musky scent of sage and piñon.

"So, how old are you tomorrow?" March asked. "If'n you don't mind me askin'."

Lane had been drinking steadily and his voice was slurred. But the man was still as alert as a hawk, the Greener handy across his lap.

"Thirty years, Rance." He shook his head; then his words betrayed his growing drunkenness. "And I've led a sinful life, killing, robbing, whoring, and raping wherever an' whoever I could."

He pointed an admonishing finger at March. "But don't you go saying I had a bad mother, because I didn't. She was a whore with a heart of damned gold, my ma. An' she went to church every Sunday and she, bless her"—Lane hiccupped—"always kept her legs crossed on the Sabbath."

"Sounds like a fine woman," March said.

Tears started in the deputy's eyes. "She was, an' don't you say otherwise. . . . Don't you say anything bad about my ma."

"I wouldn't dream of it, Hamp. Is the dear lady still with us?"

"I dunno. She left me when I was ten, an' I don't know where she went. She went somewhere, old-timer." Lane tapped the side of his nose with a forefinger. "I know that. She went somewhere."

"Let's have another drink, Hamp," March said. "We'll drink to your sainted ma."

"Tha's right, Rance. A damned saint." Lane took a long pull from the jug, wiped his mouth with the back of his hand, and said,"Held a pea between her knees on the Sabbath. Did I tell you that?"

"Yes, you did," March said. "A woman of great virtue."

Lane was aware that the jug was getting lighter, and now he kept it to himself, cradling it against his chest.

As he drank more, he was unaware that March's gaze was on him constantly—his eyes unblinking, burning in the night like those of a stalking predator.

March pretended a tipsiness he didn't feel.

"Hamp, ol' pal," he said, "can I tell you the most . . . the most sinful thing I ever done?"

The deputy's face lit up. "With a woman?"

"With three of them. Respectable, married women, mind you, but . . ."

"Wait." Lane drank from the jug, wiped his mouth again. His voice eager, he said, "Now tell me."

March moved, his leg irons clanking. He shook his head. "Naw, you're too young. You ain't ready fer a story like that."

"I ain't too young. I'll be thirty tomorrow. Tell me what you done to them women."

"I done a lot. They tired me out so, I was laid up for a week afterward."

"Damn it, tell me."

March affected a pained expression and inclined his head toward Booker. "I don't want him to hear."

"Why not?" Lane said. "Hell, you'll both be dead soon, so it don't matter none."

"I know, Hamp. But, in my last hours, it's a story I'd only tell to a friend like you."

Hamp nodded. "Well, I can take care o' that right now." He started to raise the shotgun. But March's voice stopped him.

"No, Hamp, don't kill him. I don't want you to get into any trouble with the Gravedigger."

That penetrated the deputy's whiskey-soaked brain. "Yeah, you're right. He's right set on burying you rannies alive."

"I tell you what—I'll whisper."

March leaned closer to Lane.

"Well, how it come up, the youngest of the three—"

"Wait, damn it. I can't hear you."

"Then come nearer, Hamp. I don't want to shout about the brass bed and the perfumed oil. . . ."

Whiskey and lust had dulled Lane's instinct for danger. It had blurred the line between his respect for March the gunfighter and his contempt for March the man.

Contempt in any form is a weapon of the weak, and it would cost Lane his life.

The deputy pushed closer to March, grinning in anticipation, a hand massaging his groin.

March put his mouth close to Lane's ear, whispering erotic nonsense, and his hand closed on the revolver in his pocket.

He eased back from Lane a little, and the deputy followed.

"What did she do then, huh?"

"I'll tell you the rest of the story in hell," March said.

He pushed up with his right arm, jammed the .38 under Lane's chin, and pulled the trigger.

The bullet ranged upward, tore through the soft tissue of the mouth cavity, then crashed through the fragile bones at the front of the deputy's face. The .38 slug blasted out the top of Lane's skull and blew the hat off his head.

As he jerked back, the deputy's eyes revealing his outrage at the manner and time of his dying, March shoved the gun into the middle of the big man's chest and fired again.

Chapter 18

Hamp Lane screamed and Booker could never figure out why.

It was not from pain. He was already dead, his brains scattered, yet he screamed.

Did he glimpse a terror that lay ahead for him beyond death? Or was it just his body shutting down, his soul fleeing, shrieking like steam escaping a boiler?

Amid the racketing silence that followed the last gunshot, Booker was sickened by the mode of Lane's death. He had not died like a man, but like a steer led to slaughter.

There had been no heroism in his dying, neither from him nor from Ransom March.

Booker blinked, doubts stacking up in his mind like cordwood.

Foremost and worst among them, the fact that March had not helped civilize the West with his courage, derring-do, and flashing Colts. Instead, he'd been an important part of the barbarism, of the raw, dirty, violent, and criminal West that no one wanted to read about.

Suddenly Booker had no hero and no story, and all the creative writing in the world would not change that.

He realized then that some history simply couldn't be altered.

He looked at March, a man who killed as he whispered a dirty story into his victim's ear.

Lane had been a bleeder, and the old lawman's face and hands were splashed with blood that looked black in the gloom.

March's lips were moving . . . talking to him.

"Huh?" Booker said.

"Damn it, Lester, are you deef? Get him off me," March said. "Son of a bitch weighs a ton."

Booker dragged the dead man off March, who said "Go through his pockets. We got to find the key to the padlock."

But a search of Lane turned up nothing.

"Bastard left it in the cabin," March said. He unbuckled the deputy's gun belt. "On your feet, Lester."

"What are we going to do?"

"See if we can blow the padlock apart."

Booker rose; then he and March shuffled toward the granite rock, their chains clanking in the quiet.

They were in luck, or so it seemed.

The padlock was large but crude, of forged iron, not steel, and looked as though it had been made by a town blacksmith somewhere.

"The bullet may bounce, Lester," March said, "so stand back as far as you can."

Booker stepped back as far as the slack on the chain

would allow. March thumbed back the hammer on Lane's Colt and fired at the padlock.

The bullet hit the iron and whined into the night.

The padlock had been dented, but still held fast. March swore, then fired again.

This time the round penetrated the lock, leaving a jagged hole in the wrought iron.

"We're getting someplace, Lester," he said.

He fired again, and again the bullet ricocheted, chipping granite from the top of the rock.

March looked at Booker. "Tell you something, Lester. If I ever find the son of a bitch who made this, I'll shoot him in the belly." He waved a hand. "Stand back. I'll try again."

He fired, damaging the lock, but Booker fell to the ground, groaning.

"What the hell happened?" March said, looking at him.

"I'm hit," Booker said. "Your damned bullet hit me."

"Where?"

"Left leg, damn it."

March kneeled beside Booker. Dark blood had already spread over his thigh, and the reporter's teeth were clenched against pain.

After he ripped Booker's pants away from the wound, March said, "Missed the bone, but the lead is still in there."

"I need a doctor," Booker said. "And a hospital."

"Yeah, well, we don't have any o' them around these parts," March said.

"Then I'll die. I'll bleed to death."

"No, you won't. As soon as I free the padlock, I'll cut the ball out of there. I've done it a dozen times."

Booker turned his suffering face to the indifferent moon. "I made this trip for nothing, and now I'm shot through and through and likely to die. It was a waste, all a waste."

March punched out empty shells from the Colt and began to reload from Lane's gun belt.

"I never took you fer such a complaining man, Lester," he said.

"Get me the hell out of here," Booker said, his voice rising, edged with hysteria.

"Soon as I'm done with the padlock, I'll fix you up. Then we'll lay for the Gravedigger and his boys."

Booker couldn't believe his ears. "What did you say?"

"I said I'll fix up your leg."

"After that. What did you say after that?"

"What did I say?"

"You said we'd lay for the Gravedigger and his boys."

"Right. That way we don't have to chase him any longer. Take care of the burying son of a bitch right here."

"I'm shot," Booker yelled, struggling to sit up. "And you pulled the trigger. I need to see a doctor as soon as possible."

"Lester, sometimes all a man can do is take his hits, bite back the pain, an' keep on a-comin'."

"Damn you, March. Why did you let me come here? You knew what kind of man you were. Damn you. Why didn't you tell me and save me a trip?"

March thumbed shells into the Colt.

"Lester," he said, his face empty, "seems to me that the only man who's a disappointment here is you."

He turned his back and walked to the rock, leaving Booker to stare into darkness as silent as stone.

Chapter 19

It took nine rounds for March to finally blow the padlock apart and free the chains.

He studied the shattered pieces of iron closely, then looked at Booker. "Nah, can't find a name. Pity, I'd surely like to gun that damned blacksmith."

March lifted Booker to his feet. "Lean on me and I'll help you back to the cabin. The key to the ankle shackles will be there someplace."

"I can manage," Booker said, his lips thin and white in the gloom.

"Suit yourself, Lester. But we'll have to drag the chains with us. They're heavy, like."

Booker's answer was to step toward the cabin, the chains dragging after him, reminding March of the ghost of Jacob Marley in Mr. Dickens's Christmas novel he'd read one time. Good book. And not so fat that it taxed a man.

March smiled to himself as he shuffled after the reporter.

Poor ol' Marley was condemned to drag along the sins of his past, but Booker hauled a heavier burden— Ransom March, the man who never was.

The key to the ankle shackles hung on a hook on the inside of the cabin door, alongside the now useless key to the padlock.

After he freed himself and Booker, March threw more wood into the potbellied stove and pushed the coffee-pot onto the hot plate.

The cabin's only furnishings were a table and two chairs, a wooden chest, and a shelf holding coffee, a sack of sugar, and a few cans of peaches, tomatoes, and beef.

March helped Booker into one of the chairs. "Be right back, Lester," he said, stepping toward the door.

"You're going to leave me here alone?" Booker cried.

"There's a corral behind the cabin. I'll check on our horses."

"I could bleed to death."

March cast a critical eye over Booker's leg. "Nah, bleeding's stopped. I'll dig out the bullet when I get back. I don't think she's too deep." He looked out the window. "Only a few hours until sunup, Lester. I'd bet-ter get going."

"Damn it, don't leave."

March opened the door. "Lester, I declare, sometimes you sound worse than a woman."

Booker watched the door close, then lifted his leg onto the table. The wound hurt like hell and he was sure he could feel the hard shape of the bullet, probably a jag-ged mushroom against the bone.

He needed a skilled doctor, not Ransom March rooting around with a bowie knife.

To the right of the door, two rifles and a shotgun were stacked in a gun rack.

Wincing against the pain, Booker rose and stepped to the rack. He took down a Winchester rifle, then opened the drawer underneath.

There was a box of .44-40s and a scattering of red shotgun shells.

Booker loaded the rifle, then shoved more rounds into his pocket.

Standing in a room that smelled of coffee, man sweat. and gun oil, he made up his mind. He would mount up, ride back to Santa Fe, and have the bullet removed.

After that, an eastbound cannonball and a return to New York where he could forget that this sorry mess had ever happened.

Booker opened the door and almost bumped into March.

"Where are you going with the rifle, Lester?" he said.

"I'm pulling out, heading for Santa Fe."

March shook his head. "You'll never make it on that leg. It will rot on you."

"I'm going back to New York. The new symphonic season starts next month and the Met has a Rembrandt exhibition that I'm anxious to visit."

"Then you'll go back standing on one leg, Lester. That is if the gangrene don't kill you first."

"I'll take my chances."

"I'm such a sore disappointment to you, huh?"

Booker's eyes met March's, then slid away.

"Yes, Rance," he said. "I'm afraid you are."

"Lester," March said, as though he were talking to a child, "being a lawman in the West is about surviving, not being a hero. Them as tried to be heroes are all dead."

He smiled slightly. "You know how a lawman survives?"

"I think I do."

"No, you don't, but I'll tell you: When a man keeps the peace, he gets his hands dirty. To survive long enough to see another dawn, a lawman needs to become as mean, dangerous, and violent as the outlaws he hunts. The lawman you hoped to find in me never existed and never will so long as men pin on a star."

"I must be on my way, Rance," Booker said.

"Here, you ain't sore that I killed Hamp Lane, are you?"

"You didn't kill him, Rance. You slaughtered him."

"Killed, slaughtered—what's the difference?"

"It's not how Ransom March, Prince of the Plains, would have done it."

March laughed. "Lester, the only way anybody could've gotten me on the damned plains was if they paid me to ride the cushions of a cannonball with a Pullman club car."

Booker eased his leg. Now that the shock was wearing off, it was paining him.

"Maybe the truth is that I came to find Buffalo Bill's Wild West Show, but discovered something else," he said. "It's not your fault, Rance. It's not anybody's fault. It's just how the frontier was, and still is."

"I'm real sorry we disappointed you, Lester," March said.

Booker had no more words that he felt were worth saying.

Lester Booker nodded to March and kneed his horse into motion.

"Take care of that leg now, y'heah?" March called after him.

Booker raised a hand, the gesture lost in the darkness that crowded around him.

Chapter 20

After Booker rode out, Ransom March made himself a quick breakfast of cold canned meat, peaches, and coffee.

He found his Colt in the chest, checked the loads, then shoved the revolver in his waistband. He took down the other Winchester from the rack, found it fully loaded, then stepped outside and saddled his horse.

As the remains of the night dappled into a gray dawn, March explored the creek just south of Big Costilla Peak all the way east to just north of Comanche Point, an area of craggy ridges, thick pine forests and grassy, hanging valleys.

He rode into the trees and built a cigarette, satisfied by what he'd seen.

Near the Point, Comanche Creek branched off the Costilla. If he needed to break from this country in a hurry, he could head south and follow the creek all the way to the Valle Vidal. Once there, a man could lose himself in meadows of tall grass and vast forests of pine and spruce.

It was a plan, and March liked it.

First, he'd gun the Gravedigger and hopefully Cass Logan and as many of their men as he could; then he'd hightail it south to the Valle Vidal and eventually back to Santa Fe and his ranch.

He'd be sitting pretty.

Except for one thing . . .

With both the Gravedigger and Logan dead, the location of the Spanish gold would be lost forever.

March stubbed out his cigarette on the heel of his boot and tossed away the cold butt.

That damned treasure was something for him to think about. Give him pause. Golden dreams nagged on a man.

Hamp Lane's body still lay sprawled at the base of the ridge, his unseeing eyes open in death.

Buzzards quartered the sky and a few gold-tinted clouds reminded March that it was not yet noon.

It took him an hour to find a firing position, behind an elevated ledge of limestone standing on a gradual talus slope. The ridge was flanked by a pair of stunted junipers that offered cover, and for the next couple of hours the sun would be at his back.

March studied the place for a couple of minutes and finally nodded his approval. He tethered his horse about fifty yards away in a stand of pines, and slid the Winchester from the boot.

But when March scrambled up the slope and settled behind the ledge, his enthusiasm waned. A hundred yards of open ground stood between him and the cabin.

He was no great shakes with a rifle, never had been,

and that hundred yards pretty much marked the outer limit of his range. Even then, scoring a hit would be a mighty uncertain thing.

Busying his hands with the makings, March decided that he wouldn't take the shot until the Gravedigger came close. Same for Logan. But if he missed either and they came after him, he would have precious little time to make the run for his horse.

March lit his cigarette.

Hell, it was no good building barricades on a bridge he hadn't crossed yet.

The sun pushed higher above the Culebra Range like a white-hot coin. Within the scope of March's vision, nothing moved, and there was no sound.

A horny toad, held sacred by the Hopi, Navajo, and Zuni, scuttled into March's thin shadow and squatted there, panting in the heat.

"You and me both," March said, grinning, his mouth dry as a stick.

Damn it all, when would the Gravedigger get here?

A few minutes later, the first vulture landed.

Wary at first, the huge bird studied Lane's corpse, looking for any sign of life that would send it flapping skyward again.

There was none. . . .

March watched, horrified, as another vulture landed, then another. He was close enough to see their black eyes, empty and cold as death.

He swore under his breath.

This he did not need.

A buzzard roosted on Lane's chest, looked around, its bare red head twisting slowly. It looked down at the body with apparent disinterest—then tore at the dead man's face.

The smell of blood and shredded flesh sent the other vultures into a feeding frenzy.

Within seconds, Lane's corpse was hidden under a heaving mass of birds, their heads diving into the meat of him, then deep into his coiled blue entrails.

March thought about firing into the birds, but dismissed the idea. If the Gravedigger and Logan were close, he'd betray his position.

The buzzards would scatter for a while . . . and then come back.

March caught a glimpse of Lane's white rib cage, the bloody mess of his skull, skin and flesh hanging in tatters.

The feast continued. . . .

The shot, when it came, surprised March.

A buzzard hissed into the air, staggered in flight, then thumped to earth. The flock rose as one, wings beating frantically to gain height. Another was smashed by a bullet and the rest scattered higher into the air, feathers falling like scorched leaves.

March looked beyond the birds to the horsemen entering the valley.

And for the first time in his life he saw the Gravedigger.

Chapter 21

Ransom March tightened his fingers on the Winchester and touched his tongue to his dry upper lip.

He'd try a shot as soon as the riders dismounted. Just one quick pot at the loathsome creature who had slaughtered his friends; then he'd run for it.

The Gravedigger rode in front of the others, a tall, scrawny man astride a massive gray. He had one foot in the stirrup. His other leg, his left, hung loose, a wooden dowel with a bone tip.

His eyes hidden behind dark glasses, dressed in a top hat and somber suit of black broadcloth, he looked like hell's undertaker.

Cass Logan rode behind the Gravedigger, and after him a dozen hard cases in an untidy column of twos. March recognized English McGill by his shoulder-length hair and the man riding beside him, grayer than March remembered, was Fred Kelley, the Valverde gunfighter.

Taking up the rear walked a couple of Mexican peons, their necks roped together, the end of the rope held by one of Logan's deputies.

The Gravedigger was clean-shaven, his skin the color of ancient parchment, the lines in his face carved deep, wrought by a lifetime of cruelty, violence, and madness.

March remembered a story told to him by an old-timer—he'd forgotten when or where—that the Gravedigger himself had been buried alive.

"Got hisself hung by vigilantes for a killin' down Texas way. When he was cut down, a drunken sawbones said he was as dead as a doornail," the oldster said. "They planted him deep in a pine coffin, but then, three days later, a big rain came an' caused a flood that washed out the graveyard."

The old man's eyes had taken on a faraway look. "When they found the Gravedigger's coffin, it burst open an' he was still alive. That was six days after he'd been buried. Well, the vigilantes said it wasn't decent to hang a man twicet, so they let him go."

Now March remembered that the old-timer's voice had shaken, the words clotting in his throat. "Mister, no man lives three days under the ground, then another three in the coffin."

He'd dropped his voice to a whisper. "No mortal man, that is."

March had not set much store by the old man's story, but now he saw the Gravedigger draw rein on his horse . . . and his skin crawled.

The monster was looking right at him.

He couldn't see the man's eyes, shrouded by dark glasses, but he felt the Gravedigger's gaze on him, like an icy draft from a broken window.

The Gravedigger smiled.

March swallowed hard. He was well hidden. There was no way . . .

He slowly brought the rifle to his shoulder.

Logan rode in front of the Gravedigger and said something to him.

The man shook his head, seemed angry, then waved up the riders behind him.

Damn it, they all had to dismount.

March needed the precious seconds they would use up getting back into the saddle. His horse was fifty yards away and he was not as spry as he used to be. It would take him some time to cover that ground.

Dismount, you sons of bitches. Dismount.

It didn't look like the Gravedigger had alerted Logan to his presence. Maybe the man had looked his way, but hadn't seen him.

But he'd smiled. Why?

March looked over the rifle sights, waiting for his shot. His gut was churning and he felt something akin to fear.

No mortal man, that is . . .

He pushed the words out of his mind. The Gravedigger could die like any other man.

Now the riders swung out of the saddle and March tensed.

But the Gravedigger was stepping among them and there was no chance for a clear shot.

Dragging the Mexican couple behind them, the Gravedigger, Logan, and half a dozen men broke away from the rest and walked toward Lane's corpse. Tattered scraps of meat fluttered on the deputy's scraped bones like scarlet moths.

The Gravedigger looked down at the body for long moments; then his head lifted and he turned his head in March's direction, his dark glasses flashing sunlight.

Again March felt a chill.

Damn! Had he been spotted?

By accident or design, the Gravedigger never made himself an open target. He was always partly shielded by another man's body and March did not have enough confidence in his rifle skill to pick him off.

The Gravedigger pointed to the body, said something to Logan, and both men laughed. He might have been disappointed that the deputy was dead and his prisoners gone, but the Gravedigger was obviously not grieving the man's loss.

Four men, bearing shovels, walked from the cabin. The Gravedigger immediately put them to work digging two holes in the sandy ground.

They buried the Mexican man first.

Horrified, fascinated, March watched.

He no longer planned on trying a shot. The Gravedigger, Logan, and their gunmen were too close.

He had no idea how old the Gravedigger was. The man could be fifty or five hundred, but the rest were young men and even on foot they'd run him down before he reached his horse.

The taste of defeat was like dry ashes in his mouth. March watched as the Mexican's hands were tied behind his back and he was thrown, facedown, into his grave.

The man screamed, screamed over and over, shrill shrieks of sheer terror that shattered the afternoon silence.

But there was worse, much worse, to come.

Chapter 22

The woman was slim, pretty, no older than twenty.

Like her husband, her hands were tied and she was dragged to the Gravedigger by Logan. The man smiled at her, showing teeth, and for a brief moment March thought he'd turn her loose.

But the Gravedigger roughly spun her around so that she was facing the grave. He ripped the embroidered peasant blouse from the woman's shoulders, then nodded to his waiting men.

Three of them immediately began shoveling dirt into the grave, and the Mexican man's screeches grew louder and shriller, splintering into the air like broken glass.

The Gravedigger bit down hard.

His teeth closed on the woman's glossy brown shoulder, his head jerking, savaging her. She screamed and tried to twist away, but the Gravedigger had his arms around her waist, clamping her in an iron grasp.

The cries from the man in the grave grew less, muffled by dirt and sand, but the Gravedigger bit again and again, his hungry mouth slithering up the woman's slender neck.

Her eyes huge with fear, the woman fought for her life. As a child, she'd have been told stories of the *Civatateo*, the vampire who attacks women and children, its head a bare skull.

Now she was living that horror.

The Gravedigger lifted his mouth from the woman's throat, and again, his blank eyes moved in March's direction.

The man lifted his head, his lips stretched in a grotesque grin, blood from his mouth running down his chin.

Instinctively, the gunmen watching him shrank back, including the lethal Fred Kelley. Border trash who had killed, robbed, and raped and never suffered a sleepless night, they'd seen something beyond even their experience and it horrified them.

The Gravedigger made an animal sound that even at a distance March could hear, a breathy, "Hnuh . . . hnuh . . . hnuh . . ."

"You son of a bitch," March whispered.

Had Martha Brewster suffered like this, savaged by a wild animal in human form, before she died?

March made a decision. If he let this go he would no longer be able to hold his head high in the company of men. He'd take his chances on reaching his horse before the Gravedigger's men came after him.

He raised the Winchester.

The woman was shielding the Gravedigger, and March couldn't trust his aim to score a clean head shot.

He rubbed the back of his hand across his dry mouth.

All right, he'd kill the woman, put her out of her misery.

March nestled the butt of the rifle against his shoulder, aimed between the woman's bloody breasts.

He took up the slack on the trigger, holding his breath for the shot.

But he never fired.

"Oh no," he whispered, "not now."

He lowered the rifle.

"Damn you, Lester," he whispered. "Damn your skinny hide to hell."

Chapter 23

Lester Booker was unaware of his world, his body ravaged by fever.

He was going home—he knew that—home to where someone would help him and make the heat and the pain go away.

The horse led him. Like Booker, it was heading back to remembered comfort, a warm barn, oats in the bucket, hay in the stall.

Booker nodded in the saddle. He didn't remember giving up his quest to reach Santa Fe; that had happened around the time the fever took him.

Like a wounded animal he sought shelter, a healing hand.

Not from Ransom March, but from his mother.

He looked around but couldn't see her house, the gingerbread two-story with the flowers out front and the red Rome apple trees in the backyard.

"Mother," Booker said aloud, "I'm home and I need you real bad."

Now he saw unshaven faces around him, and Booker looked to see if his editor was among them.

"Mr. Erickson, are you there?" he said.

One of the men, tall, young, a star on his chest, grinned and said something Booker could not understand.

"Huh?" he said.

Now the young man's blue eyes were angry. "I said, get off your horse."

That much Booker understood. These men were neighbors of his mother and they were going to help him.

He smiled. "Thank you."

Booker tried to step out of the saddle, but couldn't make it and settled back into the leather with a thump, his head spinning.

"Oopsy-woopsy," he said, grinning at the neighborhood stalwarts, respectable businessmen and professionals all.

The tall young man with the star grinned back at him—then drew back his fist and slammed it into Booker's bloody thigh.

Booker screamed and toppled off the horse.

Before he drowned in a scarlet sea of pain, he heard the tall young neighbor say, "I told you to get off your damned hoss, Archibald."

Ransom March made the quick determination that Lester T. Booker, late of New York City, was an idiot, then turned his attention back to the Gravedigger.

The man had watched the commotion that Booker's arrival had caused, and now he pushed the woman in front of him toward the yawning grave.

March couldn't tell if she was alive or dead. Her throat was torn, but her eyes were open wide, thin rills of blood crimson and wet on her breasts.

He couldn't take the chance. He would not let her be buried alive.

His left hand dug into the woman's hair, the Gravedigger laughed, his scarlet-stained mouth agape, as he pushed her forward.

As he had done before, March laid the irons on the woman's chest.

This time he pulled the trigger.

The bullet hit the woman clean and she dropped.

The Gravedigger was exposed.

March aimed, fired, missed.

Moving with surprising speed for a man with a peg leg, the Gravedigger loped for the empty grave. He jumped inside as March's third shot kicked up a useless exclamation point of dirt behind him.

Now March was under fire.

The scattered gunmen had him spotted, aiming into the breezeless, hanging smoke around his position.

Bullets rattled into the junipers and whined off rock, one clipping close enough that it drove chips of limestone into March's cheek, drawing blood.

Working the Winchester from his shoulder, he drove a couple of rounds in the general direction of the Gravedigger's gunmen, then jumped to his feet and ran.

March covered the ground quickly, the yells of men and probing gunshots close on his heels.

He was only five yards from his horse when disaster struck.

Chapter 24

A random bullet burned along the big stud's rump and the horse reared and broke free of its tether.

March watched helplessly as his mount vanished into the trees, crashing through underbrush in a blind panic.

"Turn around, Rance," a voice said behind him.

March turned slowly. Colt in hand, Fred Kelley stood a few yards away, a man to be reckoned with.

"Shuck the irons or I'll drop you where you stand," Kelley said.

There was no give in the man and March wasn't about to test him. He opened his fingers and let the Winchester fall.

"Now the Colt's gun."

The revolver thudded beside the rifle.

"You going to let him bury me, Kelley?" March said.

"If that's what he wants."

"A helluva thing to do to a man, and low-down."

"Well, it won't be a thing of my doing."

"I never took you fer a man who would ride with trash."

Kelley smiled. "Rance, times change and there ain't anything left for men like us. This ain't much, but it's all I got."

"Suppose I just walk into the trees?"

"Then I suppose I'll kill you." Kelley let his words hang in the air.

After a moment of mentally weighing his chances, March said,"I guess you would at that."

"You guess right."

Cass Logan stepped beside Kelley, English McGill with him.

"You got him, Fred. Good man."

"His hoss ran away," Kelley said. The gray at his temples and the tiredness in his eyes betrayed his age.

Logan grinned. "But March won't. The Gravedigger wants him real bad."

"Logan," March said, "you ain't no kind of a lawman. You're a yellow-bellied, lying dog and your diseased mother was a soldier's whore."

The sheriff shook his head and grinned. "It ain't that easy, old-timer. You won't draw a bullet from me."

He stepped forward and drove his fist into March's belly.

The old lawman doubled over and Logan's knee crashed into his face.

March fell on his back, his face bloody, and Logan stepped closer to put the boot into his ribs.

"That's enough, Cass. Leave him be."

Logan turned, his eyes ugly. "You giving me orders, Kelley?"

"He's had enough. He was a good man in his day."

Kelley didn't expect it. He never saw his death coming.

Suddenly Logan's gun was in his hand, firing.

Hit hard, Kelley took a step back, trying to bring his Colt to bear. He had taken his hit and was still standing, full of fight.

But English McGill put the period at the end of the last sentence of Fred Kelley's wild, violent life.

The breed's shotgun roared and Kelley went down, most of his belly blown out.

Logan walked to the man's body and he pumped shot after shot into him.

"I don't take orders from a hired hand," he said, talking into the fading echoes of his gunfire.

March was on the ground, holding himself up on one elbow.

"Logan," he said, through pulped lips, "you just killed a better man than you'll ever be. Twenty years ago you wouldn't have cleared leather."

Logan smiled. "Maybe so, old-timer, but he's dead and I'm alive. Me, I'm the man who shot Fred Kelley."

"Give me a gun, Logan," March said. "Let's me and you get to our work and shoot it out right now."

"March, you're pissing into the wind. Killing Ransom March ain't gonna add to my reputation." He looked at English McGill. "What do you think, breed?"

McGill shrugged. "Ransom March? Who the hell's he and who the hell cares?"

Logan nodded. "You heard it, old man. It seems you ain't worth killing. Now get on your feet. You got an appointment with a gravedigger."

Chapter 25

The Gravedigger was sprawled over the fresh graves, his head bent to one side, ear to the ground.

"They're calling to me," he said. "They wish to join me."

He scrambled to his knees and extended his arms over his head.

"Soon I will raise the dead and they will be my willing slaves for all eternity."

The man looked from Logan to March and back again. "What is this?" he said.

Logan grinned. "More worm bait for you, Gravedigger."

"This is the man who desecrated my graves and dug up the Mexican woman?"

"The very same," Logan said.

"Then you will meet her fate. I will bury you deep until the time comes for me to resurrect you."

"You go to hell," March said. "You're loco."

The Gravedigger's glasses looked like black coins on

the eyes of a corpse. "You talk to me of hell?" he said. "I've been in hell. I've seen hell."

The man's face was white, the wrinkles deep as knife scars. When he drew closer to March, his breath smelled like carrion. "What is it like to wake in the grave?" he asked.

March said nothing.

"What is it like to wake in somber darkness and feel the walls of the coffin pressing close? What is it like to scream and scratch at the lid until your fingernails are torn away? What is it like to smell the putrefied earth, the nearness of rotting corpses? What is it like to suffer the vigilant worms that slime and slither over your face?"

The Gravedigger grabbed March by the shirt and pulled him close. "What is it like?" His voice was a shriek.

Again March said nothing.

"You do not know!" the Gravedigger said. "But I do, and soon you will know also. I will teach you the secrets of the grave."

Despite the beating he'd taken, March managed to stretch his bloody mouth in a grin. "Mister," he said, "your banjo ain't tuned right. In other words, you're damned crazy."

The Gravedigger raised his hands, and made a gesture in the air of pushing March away from him.

He stood like that for a few moments; then he looked at Logan. "Where is Kelley?"

"He tried to let the old man escape and I shot him."

"Is he dead? Stone dead?"

Logan nodded. "As dead as he's ever gonna be."

"Pity."

"What do we do with him?" Logan asked. "Or have you had enough burying for one day?"

"I grow weary and the woman's blood was thin." He waved a white, blue-veined hand. "Take him to the cabin with the other one. Their time will come tomorrow."

Logan hesitated, and the Gravedigger said,"What ails you that you do not obey me?"

"When the hell do we go for the gold?"

The Gravedigger smiled. He looked like an amused cadaver. "Logan—Sheriff Logan, I should say—draw down on me."

Logan looked puzzled.

"Draw your revolver as fast as you can, as though you were going to shoot me in the belly."

Logan shrugged. "All right, you're the boss."

His hand blurred as he went for his Colt.

The Gravedigger's left hand shot out like a striking rattler and grabbed Logan's gun as it cleared the holster. His right, even faster, grabbed the lawman's throat, his clawed fingers digging deep.

Logan convulsively triggered his gun. The bullet kicked up dirt at the Gravedigger's feet.

"I say when we go for the gold," he said. The man's taloned fingers clawed deeper. "Is that clear to you, Logan?"

His frantic eyes flashing fear, the sheriff tried to speak but strangled on the words.

"Is it clear?" the Gravedigger said.

Logan nodded. He knew he was very near to death.

The Gravedigger relaxed the pressure of his fingers on the lawman's throat. He smiled. "Good. Then we are perfect friends again." He waved toward March. "Now take him away."

The skin of Logan's throat was bright red, arcs of raw flesh where the Gravedigger's fingernails had dug deep.

The lawman struggled for breath as he pushed his prisoner toward the cabin.

As March stumbled away, the Gravedigger called after him.

"What is it like to feel sunlight burn fire into the eyes after escaping the darkness of the grave?"

March walked on, not looking back.

"What is it like?" the Gravedigger shrieked.

"Your boss is nuts, Logan," March whispered.

"I know," the sheriff said, his face rigid.

"What do you plan to do about that?"

"After I get the gold, I'll kill him." He looked at March. "It's no concern of yours because you'll be dead by then."

"Why did he bite the Mexican woman until she bled?"

"I don't know."

"Does he like the taste of blood?"

"How the hell should I know? Now shut your trap."

Behind them, the Gravedigger's scream echoed, "Ransom March! What is it like? Tell me!"

Chapter 26

Lester Booker was in a bad way.

Racked by fever, he was barely conscious. His pale cheeks were flushed, rouged like those of a fifty-cent whore, and his breath came in short, tortured gasps.

The day had not yet shaded into evening, but the cabin was angled with shadow, the air inside close and stuffy, smelling of blood and sickness.

Booker lay on his back, sweat beaded his forehead, and his open eyes glittered. His lips moved, whispering, talking to someone only he could see.

March kneeled beside him and sniffed the wound on his thigh.

"Good news, Lester," he said, knowing the man couldn't hear him, but glad to toss words into the stifling silence. "It ain't rotten. At least, not yet it ain't."

Booker stirred, groaned, and for a moment his eyes met March's. But his gaze held nothing, only the bright glow of fever.

"I'm going to dig the bullet out, Lester," he said. "And

pardon me fer putting it into you in the first place." He shook his head. "You're surely a trial to me, boy."

March had never been searched and he still possessed three things precious to him: the makings, the Smith & Wesson with three live rounds still in the cylinder, and a Barlow folding knife.

After a prayer of thanks for the arrogant stupidity of outlaws, March ripped Booker's pants away from the wound.

He opened the Barlow. "I'm going to cut now, Lester," he said. "Be a brave little Yankee."

The shadows in the cabin were growing darker and March lit the oil lamp. He thought it might draw the ire of Logan and his men, but no one came near.

March cut deep, probing for the bullet.

The knife's high-carbon steel blade was rough and unpolished, but it was razor sharp and cut well.

Digging deep, March scraped bone, moved the blade slightly to his right, and cut again.

Booker stirred as pain registered on his subconscious. He dreamed of knives.

The .38 slug was a half inch from the bone, buried in thick muscle. His hands bloody, March worked the bullet out of Booker's leg, then grabbed it in his strong fingers and pulled it free.

"I got it, Lester." He grinned, holding up the .38 between his thumb and forefinger. "She was deep all right."

Booker groaned and said nothing.

"Wish we'd brung ol' Hamp's whiskey jug," March said. "I'd pour some on your wound." He sighed. "But we left it out there like a pair of eejits."

Only now did March turn his thoughts to escape.

"You're a loon because of the fever, Lester," he said, "so you don't know nothing. But as of right now, we're a couple of dead men." He smiled. "What's your opinion on that?"

Booker lay still and unresponsive. March thought his color looked better, getting back to its old ashy gray self. But that might just have been a trick of the light.

He rose to his feet, his knees snapping, walked to the cabin window, and looked outside. He saw only darkness.

March moved to the door, then stood and listened.

The wind talked softly, the pines rustled . . . and a man was crying.

Startled, March opened the door and stuck his head outside.

English McGill and another gunman stood in front of the cabin.

McGill saw March, seemed about to speak, but grinned and looked back toward the mountain.

As March's eyes became accustomed to the darkness and an aborning moon spread a thin mother-of-pearl light, he made out the shadowy figure of a man kneeling on the dead woman's grave.

The Gravedigger wailed at the top of his lungs, fists pounding on the grave, his voice bubbling through tears.

March couldn't make out all the man was saying, but it sounded like a plea to the woman that she should join him and share her blood.

"Hey, English," March said, "ain't you gonna shoot that crazy son of a bitch?"

McGill grinned. In the moonlight he looked more Kiowa than white man. "A lot of men have tried. The Gravedigger is still alive."

"Any man can be killed," March said.

"Maybe. Maybe not." McGill motioned with his shotgun. "Get back inside. You got a buryin' to attend tomorrow morning."

Chapter 27

Booker was feeling pain, and March took it as a good sign.

"Are you still a loon, or can you understand me?" he said.

Much of the heat had left Booker's cheeks, and his eyes were no longer as fevered.

"What happened to me?" he asked.

"You got shot, then tried to reach Santa Fe. You wanted to find a doctor."

"I remember I turned back. I was going home."

"You're far from home, boy."

"Where am I?"

"Still in the shadow of Costilla Peak and in a heap o' trouble."

Booker tried to sit up, failed, and sank back to the floor. "We're back where you killed Hamp Lane?" he said, his head spinning.

"The very place."

March put his arm around Booker's back and raised him to a sitting position.

"We got to get away from here, Lester, and afore daybreak at that."

"Why?"

"Because the Gravedigger is fixin' to bury us."

"I can't go anywhere," Booker said. "I'm weak and I'm burning up, damn it."

"Well, seems to me you got a choice, Lester: burn up or get buried alive. Which one o' them do you prefer?"

Booker looked around him. "We're in the cabin?"

"Yeah, and English McGill is outside with another hard case. Neither of them boys is anybody's idea of a bargain."

"I thought I was home. I thought I was at my ma's house."

March rose to his feet, irritation riding him.

"Lester, I ain't your ma." He looked down at Booker. "And let me tell you something: Right now I wish to God you were any kind of a man."

Ransom March sat on the floor, his back against the wall, thinking things through.

Fred Kelley was dead; so was Hamp Lane. English McGill and another man stood outside the cabin. That left Logan, the Gravedigger, and ten other men unaccounted for.

Where the hell were they? Camped close to the ridge or near the cabin?

He shifted his weight, easing the pain of his arthritic right hip.

If he broke out, he'd have three shots left in the Smith & Wesson, enough to take care of English and the other man.

But the light was bad, he'd be running, and McGill was good with a scattergun. He'd no idea about the second guard, but chances were he was gun-handy.

March rolled, then lit a cigarette.

His illusions left him as he smoked.

The odds were stacked against him. The hard reality was that he'd die out there in the dark. But it was better than the fate that awaited him if he did nothing.

By nature and inclination, March was not a praying man. But he raised his eyes heavenward, smiling at his presumption. He was about to ask a favor of God, but had never done anything to merit one.

Just make it quick, Lord, huh? No funny stuff like gut-shooting or anything like that.

He rose to his feet, feeling the aches of age, and took the .38 from his pocket.

Now to get the damned thing over with.

One way or another.

Chapter 28

"What are you doing?" Booker asked.

"I'm gonna shoot it out with English and them."

"I'll do it."

Tiny white moths fluttered around the orange flame of the oil lamp, and blown pine needles ticked on the cabin's tin roof.

"Lester, I'm going out there to die," March said. "There ain't no walking away from this one."

"You don't have to die."

"How do you explain that?"

"I'll do the shooting." Booker saw the puzzled expression on March's face and said,"They don't respect me. Therefore they don't fear me. They won't see it coming." He smiled. "Besides, I'm half out of my mind with fever. If I live long enough, I won't even remember it."

March smiled. "You really think you can down two gunmen with three shots? Hell, boy, English McGill is a handful all by himself."

"He'll let me get close."

"Close enough to kill you, you mean."

March stepped closer to the door, lamplight glinting off the blue barrel of the Smith & Wesson.

"Damn you, Rance, you said you wished to God I was a man," Booker said. "Well, I want to play the man's part. Now help me to my feet."

March considered that.

After a few moments he smiled. For him, the smile was reasonably warm and genuine.

"All right, Lester, I guess every man has the right to stand on his feet and die with his head high and a fire in his belly." He helped Booker up, watched him sway as his head spun, then said,"You ready?"

"Yes, give me the revolver."

"I'll do the shooting, Lester."

"English McGill won't let you close, Rance."

"I know. And I reckon that's why we're going to die tonight."

A man can play only the cards fate deals him, an axiom Ransom March would think about later.

Even as he and Booker reached the door, it burst inward, and English McGill stood framed in the doorway, the Greener pointed at March's belly.

He grinned. "Saddle up, boys. We're pulling out," he said.

McGill's eyes settled on the gun in March's hand.

"Toss away the stinger, Rance," he said, "or I'll cut you off at the knees. You'll recollect that I'm not a man who sets much store by old times."

There's a golden rule of gunfighting that says never buck a sawn-off shotgun at arm's length, and March had studied up on it.

He threw the Smith & Wesson into a corner. "Where are we going, English?" he said.

"A place."

"A place where?"

"A place where the padres' gold is hid." He motioned with the Greener. "Now outside afore I forget what a nice feller I am." He looked at Booker. "You too, Archibald."

March hesitated, trying to make sense of what was happening. "Why take us?"

"Because the Gravedigger wants it that way."

"Damn it, English, it's pitch-black out there."

"The Gravedigger can see in the dark. He'll ride point."

McGill's smile slipped from its place. "Now, both of you, out. My talking is done."

Chapter 29

March and Booker rode together, wary gunmen in front and behind them. Logan was in the lead with the Grave-digger and English McGill took the drag, covering their back trail.

Throngs of stars glittered across the vast sweep of the sky. A sighing wind explored among the arroyos and canyons and broke like an invisible tide against the craggy ridges and high peaks of the scarred land.

The column rode south through darkness, but by the time the riders reached Apache Peak, the night was shading into day. To the east, ominous and threaten-ing, an iron mass of cloud climbed above the Cimarron Range and throbbed with gold lightning.

The Gravedigger swung due east and after he reached Clear Creek Mountain, he led the way into a narrow arroyo protected by heavy growths of pine and aspen.

There he called a halt.

Rain was falling, ticking through the trees, but one of Logan's men got a fire started and put coffee on to boil.

March and Booker huddled at the base of a piñon, guarded by two hard-faced gunmen who were long on scowls and short on conversation.

Their hands were free, but Logan had shackled their ankles together.

Booker was no longer fevered, but the wound on his thigh had bled during the ride and his pant leg was soaked with blood.

His voice was strained, his breath wheezing, as he turned to March.

"I read the book *Ransom March and the Apaches*, where you were tied to a stake, a great fire burning at your feet."

March smiled. "Well, now, I never fit Apaches."

"The book said you did."

"What else did the book say?"

"It told how you got away from the bloodthirsty savages."

"Like the ones around us now, huh?"

"Yes, just like that."

Rain drummed on March's hat and rivulets of water ran off the brim.

"How did I get away?" he said.

"The book said, 'Summoning his courage, the peerless Prince of the Plains decided on a desperate course of action ere he became another victim of Apache savagery. With one bound he was free—'"

Booker said,"I wanted to remind you about the bound."

"What the hell's a bound?"

"Another word for a jump."

"Why are you telling me this, Lester?"

"Maybe you could try it again—bound, I mean."

"Bound out of these shackles? Are you crazy?"

Booker took off his plug hat and shook it free of rain. "I just wanted to mention it as a possibility, was all."

March made a laughing sound deep in his throat. "Lester," he said, "you are a one." He was silent for a moment, then said,"Damn fever fried your brains."

The Gravedigger walked toward them through the rain, eyeless behind his dark glasses.

The man looked like a walking corpse, his skin white, teeth yellow behind a wide, thin-lipped grin.

"I trust you gentlemen are quite comfortable," he said. He shrugged. "The weather is most inclement for this time of the year."

"Where are you taking us?" March said.

"Ah, on this physical plane, to a spot the locals call Tooth of Time Ridge. There, I will bury you deep, ready for the day I resurrect you to vibrant new life."

"Mister," March said, "you're even crazier than Lester here."

"You think so, Mr. March?"

"Hell, I know so. How many people have you planted around this territory?"

"I know the figure exactly: seventeen men, eight women, and three children."

"Why did you do such a terrible thing?" Booker said.

"Are you really crazy?" the Gravedigger said. "Mr. March says you're crazy."

"I got shot in the leg and had a fever."

"Ah, good. I can't have crazy people on my Council of Rulers." The Gravedigger stroked his chin. "I'm not sure about your bullet wound, though. It could well be that we'll have to chop your leg off before you are interred."

Chapter 30

The Gravedigger dropped to a squatting position near Booker, then leaned forward as though to impart an intimate confidence.

"You see, better for you if you're resurrected with one leg. An artificial limb can be quite distinguished, as I can testify. But a bullet wound that never heals?" He shook his head. "No, not in the council."

Anger flashed in March. "What the hell are you talking about, and can we get a cup of coffee?"

"As to what I'm talking about, the dead can't die twice, hence, the resurrected will be immortal." The Gravedigger smiled. "Like me."

He stared into Booker's eyes.

"You are intelligent and talented, Mr. Booker, but I can't have you sitting on my council with a bleeding bullet wound. That would be . . . well, low class."

He put his hand on the younger man's shoulder. "No, better we chop off the offending leg. Then, when I raise you, I'll fit you with a new leg."

"What council?" Booker said. His fear made him strident. "What the hell are you saying?"

"Just this: I will use the money from the Spanish treasure to buy my way to power. Then I will form my Council of Rulers. Ha, the earth will prosper and be happy under my leadership. Never fear."

The man rose to his feet. "You two don't understand it yet, but you will be a part of it, the glory that is to come."

The Gravedigger stepped away, then turned. "As for coffee, I'll ask Logan to bring you a cup to quench your thirst."

Then, as though he'd forgotten something, he said, "Like you are now, when I lay in the grave my mouth was dry. I tried to scream for help but could not utter a sound."

He raised his hands and showed his scarred wrists.

"I bit myself until the blood flowed"—he thrust his wrists forward—"here and here. I drank that blood and felt strength surge through my body. My lungs no longer labored but thrived on the stinking air inside the coffin and I heard a voice whisper, 'You have found the way.'"

Thunder crashed above the arroyo, and lightning struck a nearby pine. The tree split open and briefly caught fire until the scarlet moths of flame, raked by the roaring rain, died into wisps of smoke.

The Gravedigger seemed not to notice.

"Both of you will soon find the way," he said, looking at March. "The wine-dark blood of some dying wretch will sustain you and, like me, you will need no other sustenance."

* * *

"Here, share this swill between you."

Cass Logan extended a smoking cup to March. "English McGill calls it coffee."

The Gravedigger had walked deeper into the arroyo, shrouded in rain and gloom.

March took the cup from Logan and the sheriff grinned. "He talking about blood again?"

"He's nuts."

"Sure is."

"When you gonna gun him, Logan?"

"Like I told you, after he leads us to the gold."

"Maybe the Gravedigger can't die," Booker said.

"Gravedigger my ass. His real name is Bill Roe and he was hung by vigilantes on May 26, 1888, for murder. Seems the fall didn't break his fool neck, but some drunken doctor pronounced him dead anyway."

"So he really was buried alive?" Booker said.

"Yeah, Archibald, he was." Logan's eyes glinted meanness. "And I reckon before much longer you're gonna find out what it's like."

"Let us go, Logan," March said. "We mean nothing to you."

"You're right, old man. You don't. But the Gravedigger sets store by you, and I won't cross him until he points the way to the Spanish gold." He smiled. "It's business, you understand."

"You're trash, Logan," March said.

The sheriff's boot shot out and kicked the coffee cup from March's hand, the boiling-hot liquid erupting into the air.

"That just cost you your morning coffee, old-timer." Logan grinned.

March watched Logan leave, then said, "I'm gonna take real pleasure in killing that man."

Booker, soaking wet and weak from his wound and the older man's crude surgery, smiled slightly. "Rance, we're both going to be six foot under soon. Difficult to shoot a man from there."

"Sorry I brung you out here, Lester," March said.

"You didn't bring me. I did it of my own free will. It was a big mistake. The last I'll ever make, I reckon."

"Well, we ain't buried yet. Damn it, boy, I'll find a way."

Booker managed a weak laugh. "Rance March, Prince of the Plains, could find a way."

"Yeah, with one bound. And me? What about me, Lester?"

"You lost your way a long time ago, Rance. Maybe the first time you shot a man in the back."

"Hard words, Lester. Maybe you should walk in my shoes first."

Booker turned to March, hoping what he was about to say hurt March as much as it hurt to say it. "Rance, your shoes are way too small for me."

Chapter 31

The Tooth of Time Ridge rose nine thousand feet above the flat like a broken canine.

Once, the sheer, rocky pinnacle marked the cutoff to the Santa Fe and Oregon trails, but now it was the point where the Gravedigger swung northwest. He led his column past Bear Mountain and then crossed the Cimarron River, low at this time of year and untroubled by white water.

They passed Cimarroncito Peak in a drenching downpour.

This was a land of silent mountains, bottomless canyons, and mythical forests. A man could lift his eyes and move from willow and cottonwood, higher to piñon, juniper, and oak, then higher still to vast stands of aspen, spruce, fir, and Engelman spruce. The grasslands were ablaze with wildflowers, mountain bluebells, sunflowers, and irises lending their beauty to dozens of others.

It was a land to lift a man's spirits, but Ransom March rode bent-shouldered in the saddle, pounded by rain, punished by doubts.

He and Booker were closely guarded and there seemed to be little hope of escape, none of rescue. The grave was yawning open at his feet, black and wet with rain, and, near as he could tell, there wasn't a damned thing he could do about it.

Behind him Booker was closeted with his own thoughts, none of them any brighter than those of March's.

His leg pained him, fear pained him, and it pained him that he'd gotten himself into this fix in the first place. Ransom March was a deeply flawed hero and all the rewriting of history wouldn't change that one, damning fact.

Booker fervently wished he'd known it earlier. Back in New York.

He turned his face to the falling rain, opened his mouth, tasted the sky.

Cass Logan watched him, then laughed.

They rode up on the farm wagon a mile south of Cimarron Canyon.

Even from a distance it was obvious that the rear axle was broken. The canvas-covered Studebaker canted drunkenly and beside it, a woman in a yellow slicker looked helplessly at the wreck.

The Gravedigger, Logan with him, kneed his horse into a canter. The woman watched them come for a few moments, then grabbed a rifle from under the wagon seat.

March watched the Gravedigger talk to the woman while keeping his distance. She listened for a while, then lowered the rifle.

March cursed under his breath.

Bad mistake, lady.

The woman turned, reached up into the wagon, and gathered a child in her arms.

It was difficult to tell at a distance, but March figured the kid was a little girl about four or five years old.

He turned and looked at Booker, knowing the man was thinking the same thing he was: two more victims for the Gravedigger.

Logan rode to the wagon, picked up the woman's rifle, then turned in the saddle and waved the rest of them forward.

When March and the others reached the wagon, Logan grinned and said,"This here is Mrs. Eliza Rowantree and her daughter, Judith. Her axle broke as you can see. Then her team bolted."

He looked at the woman, but talked to his men. "Seems Mrs. Rowantree shot her old man for trying to molest the kid and now she's headed for Santa Fe. Ain't that right, ma'am?"

The woman sensed danger. March could see it in her face. She had miscalculated these men badly.

Her fears were confirmed by the Gravedigger.

"She's pretty enough, lads," he said, talking through the woman as though she weren't there. "And ye can all have a taste. But no rough stuff, mind. I want her alive."

Three or four of the gunmen cheered and March saw hunger in their eyes.

The woman's prettiness was faded, lined by weather,

disappointment, and hard work. But even under the loose-fitting slicker, her body still seemed slim and shapely.

"We'll find a place to camp," the Gravedigger said. "I have no desire to tackle the canyon in this downpour."

"Spread out, boys. Find a place," Logan said. He waited, expecting someone to make a move. "Hell, the woman will still be here when you get back."

The men finally moved out and scattered into the foothills.

March, the oldest man there, caught the woman's eye. Was she silently pleading for his help?

If that was the case, he'd none to give her.

Six men, including Cass Logan, raped Mrs. Rowantree that night.

To March's surprise English McGill took no part in it, sitting away from the others, his face like stone.

The Gravedigger tilted his head, listened to his men grunting like hogs in the underbrush, and occasionally smiled. But he did not go near the woman.

A quiet, withdrawn child who looked constantly in the direction of the bushes but said nothing, the little girl sat between March and Booker.

Young as she was, Booker knew that the girl was aware of what was happening and he tried to distract her.

"Judith is a pretty name," he said.

The child looked at him with huge brown eyes but did not respond.

Angry at his own weakness, angry at Logan and his men, Booker took it out on March.

"Judith," he said, "would you like to hear a story?"

The girl said nothing, listening into the gasping night.

"Once there was a hero lawman who wasn't a hero at all," Booker said. "In fact he was a coward who stood by and did nothing while a woman was outraged."

March's own anger flashed. "What would you have me do, Lester?"

"Judith, do you know what the hero who wasn't a hero should have done?"

Again the child did not answer.

"He should have tried to stop it, shouldn't he?"

"And take a bullet?" March said.

"He should have stood up like a man, and sacrificed himself for the woman. That way, you see, his life might have been a lie, but his death would fit the legend and that's what people would remember. I would make them remember."

"Lester," March said, his anger cooled, replaced by faint amusement, "since you're so all fired up about saving the lady's honor, why don't you do it? And bear in mind, you're shackled to me."

Booker's face betrayed his inner torment. "Because I'm afraid, and suddenly I don't want to die. I want to see my home again."

March smiled. "Lester, for a man who wants to go back to his gray-haired mama, I'd say you're in the wrong place at the wrong time."

In the end, the Gravedigger stopped it.

When the last of the six rapists walked out of the woods, he stepped to the bushes.

"That's enough," he said. "Those who lusted for a taste got it. I want the sow alive, not rode to death."

The sixth man, a bearded giant with a scar across one eye, grinned. "Why don't you have a go, now we've greased her up for you?"

The Gravedigger ignored the man and walked into the brush. He emerged a few moments later, dragging the woman by the hair.

"Bitch clawed me," he said.

He turned his head, showing parallel red scars running from cheekbone to chin.

"Guess she didn't think much o' what you had to offer," a man yelled. Others laughed.

The Gravedigger viciously backhanded Eliza Rowantree across the face. The woman's head snapped to the side, saliva and blood flying from her mouth, and she dropped at his feet.

"Hear ye all," the Gravedigger said. "I will not raise this woman to life. I will let her lie in the grave as feed for worms."

"Hell, now we're done with her, she ain't fit fer anything else," Logan said, and men laughed again.

The Gravedigger pulled Mrs. Rowantree to her feet and dragged her to where March and Booker were sitting with the child.

He threw the woman to the ground and said, "Sit there with your get. Prepare her well for what is to come."

Chapter 32

An erratic wind shredded the rain into shards of splintered glass that hammered March with cold stings.

Beside him the woman sat, head bent, her child in her arms, making the soft, soothing sounds that women knew and men didn't.

Booker was shivering, his knees drawn up to his chest, but whether from cold or fever, March couldn't tell.

The campfire, built in the shelter of an overhang, fluttered and sizzled, spreading little light. Blanket-wrapped men had sought what shelter they could find; only English McGill was awake, the Kiowa in him enduring. Of the Gravedigger, there was no sign.

"Mrs. Rowantree," Booker said, "I'm so sorry."

The woman looked at him with dry eyes. "Sorry for what?"

"That we couldn't save you."

"Save me from what?"

"From . . . from what happened in the woods."

"If you'd tried, you'd have gotten your fool head

blown off. But thanks for the sentiment." The woman looked closely at Booker, piecing him together in the inky dark. "What's your name?"

"Lester, ma'am, Lester Booker."

She almost smiled. "Funny, I took you for an Archibald."

"It seems that many people out west make that same assumption, Mrs. Rowantree."

"Call me Eliza. That Rowantree name doesn't set well with me."

"You experienced a terrible ordeal. I'm so sorry."

"You're sorry for a lot of things, ain't you, Lester?"

Eliza held Judith closer, trying to shield her from the worst of the downpour.

"When Jeb Rowantree found me, I was working as a two-dollar whore on a hog ranch south of Santa Fe. There isn't anything a man can do to me that hasn't been done a hundred times before."

"But you were raped," Booker said. "Repeatedly."

"Good for you, Lester. Not many men think like that."

"Like what?"

"That a woman who sells her ass for two dollars can be raped."

Booker felt his cheeks burn and was grateful for the darkness.

"The man who hit me"—Eliza's fingers strayed to the bruise on her cheek—"what was he talking about, that he won't raise me to life?"

"You mean you don't know who he is?" March said.

The woman shook her head.

"He's the Gravedigger."

"Oh my," Eliza said, hugging Judith closer.

"You've heard of him?" March said.

"Jeb told me about the Gravedigger. He buries people alive, even children."

"We'll get out of this," March said.

"How?" Eliza looked around frantically. "Maybe I can throw myself on his mercy. Maybe I can beg—"

"Mrs. Rowantree . . . Eliza . . . the Gravedigger is mad," Booker said. "He has no mercy."

"I'll think of a way," March said.

"Mister," Eliza said, "that's big talk from a man with his legs in shackles and no gun."

"Why, don't you know, Eliza? This is the famous lawman Ransom March, fearless Prince of the Plains."

Booker had laid on his sarcasm with a trowel, but the woman ignored him and clasped Judith closer to her.

Above the rattle of the rain, March thought he heard sobs, but couldn't tell if they came from Eliza or the child.

Either way, he felt helpless.

Chapter 33

Booker woke, sensing that someone was watching him closely.

Soaked, shivering from the rain and the night cold, he opened his eyes.

The Gravedigger squatted in front of him, his gray hair plastered over his forehead.

"What's it like, Mr. Booker?" he asked.

Booker's brain was cobwebbed with the remains of a dream. He said nothing.

"What is it like?" the Gravedigger said again.

"What is what like?" Booker said.

"The grave."

"I don't know."

"But you will."

The Gravedigger leaned closer. "What's it like to wake in the coffin in stygian blackness?"

"Terrifying, I imagine."

"Terrifying, indeed, Mr. Booker."

The Gravedigger's eyes moved to March, then to Eliza and her daughter. "Soon you will all know."

"Let the woman and her child leave," Booker said.

"Do not be concerned. My anger has cooled and I will raise them again."

"You'll kill them. There will be no raising of the dead."

The Gravedigger pulled down the collar of his shirt. "Look," he said.

His neck bore a terrible scar, whiter than the white of his skin. "What is it like to stand on the gallows and count the seconds to the drop?"

"I don't know."

"I pissed myself."

"I'm sorry."

"The sun was full in the sky that day, and I saw a hawk, just above my head. And a washerwoman was singing down by the river."

The Gravedigger's voice grew distant as he remembered.

"Then the ground opened under my feet and I dropped into nothing. The rope jerked taut, and my head felt as though it was being torn off my shoulders. Pain that I can't describe but still feel."

His shadowed eyes glowed with fire, like hot coals. "When I woke I was in the grave."

He ran a hand through his wet hair. "Look at my hair. When I entered the grave it was black. When I was raised to new life, it had become white. White! Turned to white by terror, Mr. Booker. I bit my tongue, ground my teeth, cried for help, listened to the worms, and all the while my hair was turning white as snow."

Booker did not speak.

"What is it like?" the Gravedigger said.

"I don't know."

"You do not know."

Slowly, the Gravedigger rose to his feet. He turned and walked into the rain-lashed night.

The dawn brought an end to the rain. The clouds drew back and unveiled a copper-colored sky streaked with gold and amber.

Logan's men made coffee and fried bacon, but there was none for the prisoners.

The sun had not yet cleared the mountain peaks when they descended into Cimarron Canyon.

The Gravedigger avoided the canyon's sheer palisade cliffs and followed an easier route, a switchback game trail that led to the river below.

Eliza Rowantree, Judith sitting behind her, was mounted on a Morgan that had pulled her wagon and had been rounded up by McGill. She was pale under her tanned skin, her eyes red-rimmed and dull.

March and Booker rode side by side, the old lawman's eyes constantly searching the terrain around him.

Although his hands were tied behind him, he planned to make a break when an opportunity presented itself. So far, closely guarded and verging on exhaustion, there had been no chance.

Beside him, Booker slumped in the saddle. He looked as though he'd lost twenty pounds since arriving in the territory, a severe loss for a man who'd been as skinny as a fence post to begin with.

March was concerned enough to ask how Booker felt.

"I don't know."

"Fevered? Sick? Weak?"

"All of the above."

"Bear up, Lester. I got you into this and I'll get you out of it."

Usually that would have drawn a sarcastic retort from the newspaperman, but he said only, "I sure hope you do."

That clinched it for March. Lester was even sicker than he looked.

They passed through a dappled stand of dogwoods, then rode up on the river. Trout jumped as they crossed and March made a mental note to come back here with a fly rod—if he lived that long.

By the time the Gravedigger led the way out of the canyon, the sun blazed fair in the sky and only a few white clouds drifted above Moreno Valley to the west.

A blue grouse gave March the opportunity he'd been hoping for.

The bird burst out of the grass and fluttered between the mounts of the two riders behind him. As the gunmen fought their spooked horses, March kneed his black to the left, breaking for the rim of the canyon.

March rode fifty yards at the gallop, hugging the rim, before Logan and his men opened fire on him.

Then they came after him, riding hard, shooting as they closed the distance.

Bullets spit the air around March. Ahead of him was

another fifty yards of open ground, then a stand of mixed aspen and wild oak.

Rocking in the saddle, made unsteady by his tied hands, March headed for the trees.

He never made it.

He heard the dull thud of a bullet hit the big stud. The horse staggered under him, tried to collect itself, but cartwheeled forward and its neck broke with a sickening snap. March flew over the horse's head, slammed into the ground hard, and rolled.

Suddenly there was no longer anything solid under him.

He toppled over the canyon rim and fell . . . a tumbling plunge into thin air. . . .

Chapter 34

"Is the son of a bitch dead?"

Cass Logan sat his horse and spoke to English McGill as he peered over the canyon rim.

"Hell, I don't know. I can't see him."

"Then he fell all the way."

"Maybe so, Cass, but I ain't going down there to find out."

"You'll go if I tell you to go. But, what the hell, he's as dead as a rotten stump."

"Is he dead? Is March dead?" The Gravedigger rode up next to Logan.

"He fell over the rim," Logan said. "I reckon he took a bullet."

The Gravedigger called to McGill. "Do you see his body? Do you see March?"

"I don't see nothing. There's all kinds of trees and rocks down there and he fell a long way."

"He's dead," Logan said. He glanced at the sky. "We're wasting time."

"I wanted him," the Gravedigger said.

Logan smiled. "Well, he ain't worth anything to you now." He spoke to McGill. "Mount up. We're getting out of here."

The Gravedigger rode to the rim.

"What's it like, March?" he yelled. His voice echoed around the canyon. "What's it like?"

Ransom March opened his eyes.

Just a few feet from him, a buzzard rode an air current, flapping its wings occasionally to maintain height. The bird's cold, merciless eye appraised him, looking for signs of life.

"Get the hell away from me," March said. Despite the fall, his hat had stayed in place, and he lashed out with it.

The move unbalanced him and he almost rolled off the narrow ledge of rock that had saved his life.

He scrambled back from the edge and his back fetched up against the canyon wall. He stayed there for a while, his heart thumping wildly in his chest.

The vulture drifted away. Patient beyond belief, it knew its time was not yet . . . but would come soon enough.

March moved, testing his body, and found that he was hurting everywhere. Nothing seemed broken, but he reckoned he was bruised all over, like the last apple in the barrel.

Years of rough living had endowed March with a legacy of toughness that reached into every bone and muscle fiber of his body. He was lean as a lobo wolf and there was no softness in him. In the past he had taken blows and bullets and survived. And he was game enough to do it all again if forced to it.

A fellow law officer had summed it up, "Ransom March is a man who is hard to kill and you can bet your bottom dollar that if you brace him, you'll die trying."

But right now, March would have been hard-pressed to agree with that assessment.

The ledge where he lay was only about two foot wide and the canyon wall behind him looked sheer and impossible to climb.

He rolled on his back.

Above him, scrub brush clung desperately to the rock, some of it broken and bent, marking the direction of his descent. The brush had done little to break March's fall, but it had hidden the ledge from any searcher on the rim.

He eased himself into a sitting position, his legs drawn up. He was in one hell of a fix. There was no way he could climb a vertical rock face. One slip and he would be dead meat.

And he was worried.

The vulture had been bad enough, but now the sky was clouding again. Pinned helplessly to the rock wall of the canyon, he was a target for lightning.

He considered his options.

He could fry and die . . . fall and die . . . starve and die . . . thirst and die. . . .

That wasn't a list a man cares to choose from.

March stretched, feeling his aches, and made up his mind.

Damn it, if he couldn't climb up, he'd climb down.

He used his teeth to work on the knotted rope around his wrists. All that accomplished was to give him a toothache.

He looked around him. Above his head a narrow fissure in the rock face had not yet been worn down by time and weather, and the edges of the cleft were fairly sharp.

Slowly, taking care, he rose to his feet. He turned, faced the fissure, then rubbed the rope up and down the edge.

This was going to take time. But a rumble of thunder told him that time was a luxury he could ill afford.

Chapter 35

The old lawman was dead.

Lester Booker couldn't believe it.

Ransom March should have gone out in a blaze of glory, years before, a smoking Colt in his hand and his beard in the sawdust of a saloon floor.

For all his faults, he didn't deserve to die a dog's death.

As he and Eliza were led deeper into the mountains by Logan and the Gravedigger, Booker composed a eulogy of sorts in his mind, knowing that it was way too late to right some wrongs.

March had been a great disappointment to him, an ordinary man who spawned an extraordinary legend. Lashing out in his frustration, he had all but accused the man of cowardice.

He didn't realize until now, this minute, that true courage is not loud and boastful. It doesn't shout its name. In the final analysis it comes down to a man doing what he thinks is right, no matter the odds or the risks.

That was what drove March, but he would do it in his own way.

He had tried to wound the old lawman with sarcasm, scar his fine, quick pride.

March had tolerated it with a smile.

A man doesn't lash out at the baby who bites him. It's only a child and knows no better.

Booker realized that was how March felt about him.

He'd said things to March that would have gotten any other man killed. But the old lawman drew the line at shooting children and rubes.

Booker turned his face to the sky and his eyes stung.

Had he been that wrong?

All along, had Ransom March the raw lawman and town tamer been a better man than Ransom March, the peerless Prince of the Plains?

Booker thought he now knew the answer to that question. But the time for apologizing had come, gone, and would never return.

They camped that night north of Baldy Mountain, avoiding the boom town that had been built on the peak since gold and copper were discovered there in 1866.

There were mutterings of discontent among Logan's men, who resented that they had been denied the chance to visit Baldy's saloons and brothels.

The Gravedigger smoothed things over when he promised that they were close to the location of the Spanish gold. He also gave them Mrs. Rowantree to play with.

Booker tried to save the woman, and was severely

pounded by Logan and another man. Only when the boots started to go in did the Gravedigger put a stop to it.

His left eye closed, his sides aching from kicks, Booker sat in the darkness, his back against a tree. He held Judith in his arms, and mercifully the girl was asleep.

Around the clearing in the pines where they'd made camp, a thunderstorm raged, blades of lightning flashed into the surrounding mountains and added color to the rain.

The Gravedigger brought Booker coffee. At first he was tempted to refuse, but then swallowed his pride and accepted.

The coffee was hot, strong, and bitter and Booker drank it gratefully.

The Gravedigger watched him.

"Why?" Booker said finally.

"Are you talking about Mrs. Rowantree?"

"Yes, her. As we sit here, she's being raped."

"She's a whore."

"Not any longer."

"Once a whore, always a whore."

"Put a stop to it."

"No."

"Why not?"

"She means nothing to me. I reconsidered what I told you earlier and now I don't intend to bring her back to life. You, I will resurrect, but not her. She is an impure thing."

"Then we have nothing to talk about."

"Perhaps we don't. But I will feed on Mrs. Rowantree's blood, and her child's blood. It will make me strong for what has to be done."

The coffee in Booker's cup tasted more bitter, less good than it had tasted before.

"What has to be done?" Booker said. "Burying alive Mrs. Rowantree, this child, and myself?"

"That, and other things."

"What other things?"

"You will call it murder."

"I can stand the shock."

The Gravedigger waved a hand around the clearing. "None of these men will come out of the mountains alive. I will destroy them all."

Booker smiled, paining his split, swollen lips. "You don't even carry a gun."

"I do not need a gun." The Gravedigger leaned forward. "You can help me."

Booker saw an opportunity and took it. "I'll help you, but only if you free Mrs. Rowantree and the girl."

"Do not dictate terms to me, Mr. Booker, on peril of your life."

"Nevertheless, those are my terms."

"Then I will consider what you say." The Gravedigger grinned. His hand shot out and grabbed Booker's left wrist. His fingers tightened and Booker cried out in pain. "I can crush your bones until they turn to cornmeal," the Gravedigger said.

Booker gritted his teeth against the pain. He tried to pry the man's fingers loose, but they held like steel bands.

"Let me go, damn it," he said.

"Do you know what this is, Mr. Booker?"

Booker shook his head and grimaced, unable to talk.

"It is the strength of those who were dead but are now alive. Ah, it is a mighty strength."

He released his grip and Booker felt stinging blood rush back to his hand.

"What is it like?" the Gravedigger said.

"Painful, damn you."

"Do I need a gun?"

Booker shook his head.

"Yes, that is right. I need no gun."

The Gravedigger rose to his feet. "I will stop the hogs rutting between Mrs. Rowantree's thighs and then consider your proposition."

Chapter 36

It took an hour for March to free himself of his bonds, and by then his wrists were scraped raw, as were his nerves.

The thunderstorm was much closer, booming overhead, the lightning flashes vivid and spiteful. As yet there was no rain.

As March worked on fraying the ropes, he'd decided on a way down.

It wouldn't be easy and left a big question mark in his mind.

Five feet from the end of the ledge and twice as much lower, a talus slope formed an inverted V of shingle and chips of limestone. The incline seemed to be gradual enough for a man to slide without falling.

But then came the question mark.

The slope ended at a ridge, and beyond that he could see nothing but the rocky floor of the canyon hundreds of feet below.

What lay beyond the ridge? A sheer drop that would

break his fool neck, or did the talus slope continue un-hindered?

It was a question a man could only answer by try-ing. And trying could kill him.

Thunder crashed above March's head and now the rain started, rattling around him. Lightning struck some-where on the rim, close enough to make him cling like a leech to the rock wall.

It was time.

March took off his hat and held it in his hand. Some-how the hat had stayed on his head and he didn't want to lose it now.

He shuffled to the far end of the ledge. He'd have to leap a good ten feet before he dropped down onto the talus slope. It was no easy jump for a man who suf-fered from the rheumatisms and bore the stiff scars of ancient bullet wounds.

The rain pummeled him and lightning continued to scare all kinds of hell out of him.

March gathered himself. "All right, Rance," he said aloud. "We jump for it on three."

He stepped back as far as he could, giving himself a short run. The ledge was slick with rain, muddy and treacherous.

"One . . ."

March felt fear ball in his belly.

"Two . . ."

He bent forward slightly and placed his left foot in front of his right. His breath came in short, sharp gasps.

"Three!"

Damn! The run had been a bad idea.

March's left bootheel skidded and flew out from under him. The slip turned him around so that he hit the talus slope on his side. Then he was tumbling head over heels, cartwheeling toward the ridge.

"Oh, shiiiiiiiiiiiiit!"

He slammed into the edge of the ridge, and somer-saulted into space in a tangle of flailing arms and legs.

After what seemed an eternity, March thudded onto a hard mix of shingle, sand, and loose rock. But there he stopped.

All the wind slammed out of his body and left him gasping, struggling to get a breath into his tortured lungs.

After a couple of minutes, he struggled to his hands and knees, the taste of green bile in his throat. There was nothing in his stomach, but he vomited strings of saliva stained with blood, retching so hard his body shuddered.

March flopped on his back, letting the rain wash over him. He lay there for a long while before he struggled to his feet.

Once he was standing, the pain slammed at him.

He felt as though he had broken all his ribs, his hip, neck, both arms, and both legs. Come winter he would pay for this, lying in his bed of a morning stiff as a board, Lafe clucking and *tut-tut*ting over him like a mother hen.

To March's surprise, his hat was still clutched in his hand. He jammed it on his head and looked up at the ridge.

Damn! He'd only fallen ten feet from the ledge, but it had seemed like a hundred. He figured he'd tumbled through the air for a long time.

Suddenly he was tired, worn out. But now the way to the canyon bottom was gradual, a grassy slope thick with wildflowers.

March made his way to the flat, then walked into the dogwoods, where he found a relatively dry spot that was sheltered from the worst of the rain.

He fell on his belly, closed his eyes, and was asleep instantly.

Chapter 37

"I can't believe March is dead," Booker said. "He seemed indestructible, like he'd live forever."

"All men die," Eliza Rowantree said.

"And nothing changes. The sky is the same, and the mountains."

"The sky and the mountains don't grieve for a man's death or rejoice at his birth, Lester. They're just . . . there."

They rode in silence for several minutes; then Booker said, "I don't know how you stand it. I think I'd kill myself."

"That's because you're a male," Eliza said. "Women are taught how to endure. Nature makes them that way."

"I couldn't help you. I just sat there."

Eliza said nothing. She looked drawn, remote, but maintained a bond with her daughter, holding Judith close as she rode.

Two miles north of Baldy Mountain, the Hangman led the way east, into a land of deep, grassy valleys, forested mountains, and brooding mesas.

The dawn had brought no relief from the downpour and both Booker and Eliza were soaked to the skin. The chill of evening was gone, but though the day was hot and steamy, the black sky spread a gloom that shadowed the valleys and inked the spaces between the trees.

This was a rugged land, echoing with ancient silences, but that morning it looked like a smudged painting by a poor watercolorist who had tried but failed to capture its stunning beauty.

"Are you hungry?"

Eliza's question surprised Booker, coming out of the blue like that. "Yes, yes, I am."

"They won't give us anything to eat. Judith is hungry, but she won't complain."

"She's a quiet child."

"Yes. She doesn't say much."

Booker said,"I think I've made a deal with the Gravedigger to let you and Judith go."

Eliza turned to him. She had a cut on her left cheekbone, her mouth was bruised around the lips, and her skin was scraped red by stubbled beards. Her dress had been torn away from shoulders that were scarred by bite marks.

Yet her eyes were still alive, dark gray in the gloom of the day. "He told you he would?"

"Not yet, but he will."

"What does he want in return?"

"He wants me to stand by him when it comes time for him to make his fight against Cass Logan and the others."

The woman shook her head. "He wants more than that, more than he's telling."

"But that's all he said."

"Booker, I think you're probably a nice man, but nobody's going to choose you to side with them in a shooting scrape. Logan's men are skilled revolver fighters and they'd gun you down quicker'n scat."

The woman glanced at the sullen sky.

"The Gravedigger wants you for something, but it's not to fight for him," she said.

"It doesn't matter, so long as he frees you and Judith."

"I don't think that will happen."

"Why not?"

"Because the Gravedigger is evil. No, it's more than that. He's not human. He doesn't think and act like ordinary men."

She looked into Booker's eyes. "Have you ever seen him eat?"

"No."

"Drink?"

"Only blood." Booker looked stricken. "I shouldn't have said that. I'm sorry."

"What's in store for us? What will happen to my child?" Eliza said.

Judith was looking at Booker with eyes as big and round as silver dollars.

"Nothing. Nothing will happen to you. I'll fix it with the Gravedigger."

A bird called in the distance, defying the rain. A

man's horse snorted and tossed its head, the bit jangling.

"I wish," Eliza said, "that Mr. March was still with us."

"He had no gun," Booker said.

A directness in the woman's eyes revealed that she was not trying to wound.

"I know," she said. "But he was a man."

Chapter 38

Ransom March woke to rain.

Soaked, he rose to his feet in the watery dawn and figured he couldn't put a dime on a part of his body that didn't hurt.

At the best of times he had the horseman's stiff-kneed walk, but now as he left the dogwoods he moved as though his joints were made of rusted tin.

Head bent against the downpour, he took an hour to find the switchback he'd followed the day before.

The climb to the canyon rim exhausted him, and by then his hands and knees were abraded raw by rock and thornbushes.

The last thing in the world March needed was to reach the top and find himself staring into the muzzle of a Winchester.

But that was what happened.

"I guess this is how it transpires by times, Rance," English McGill said, grinning. "A man thinks he's free and clear, but all he's done is jump out of the fire into the frying pan."

March scrambled to his feet. "What the hell do you want, McGill?" he said.

"Nothin' much."

"Well, right now I'm half dead, so I'm hardly worth killing."

"Seems like."

"Where are the others?"

"With Logan and them."

"They still alive?"

"Last I seen. 'Course by now they might have graveled the Gravedigger real bad an' he buried them right away."

"Did you come here to make sure I was dead?"

"That's a reason, I guess."

"And now you're going to gun me?"

"No. I want to talk to you."

"Won't Logan see you're gone?"

"Nah, I always cover our back trail. Can't have folks like you sneakin' up on us."

"What do you want to talk about? The damned weather?" Rain drummed on March's hat and the sky flashed.

"A partnership, me and you."

"Then you'd better kill me and be done, English. I don't side with a son of a bitch and low person."

"Takes one to know one, Rance."

"And I don't shoot women."

"I don't either, unless I'm following orders."

McGill's yellow slicker ran with rain. "I got coffee, if'n we can find a dry spot to build a fire." He grinned. "Unless you don't drink coffee with a son of a bitch."

"You got the makings?"

"Sure enough."

"Then let's try the pines over there."

"You're a reasonable man, Rance."

"No, I ain't. Not when it comes to you. But I need coffee and a smoke."

March took the makings from McGill and started to build a cigarette.

"Keep 'em," the breed said. "I got more."

They were in a sheltered spot between the trees, but rain still dripped through the branches and occasionally a fat drop sizzled into the fire.

McGill watched March light his smoke and pick up his coffee cup.

"You ready to talk?" he said.

"It's a free country," March said. Tobacco had worked its magic, the coffee had revived him, and he felt better.

Thunder blasted and lightning flickered on the ground between the pines.

"You still sore about that woman?" McGill said.

"There was no need to kill her."

"And no need for Logan and them to screw the ass off Mrs. Rowantree, but it's happening. I don't like that, Rance. It don't set well with me."

"Strange talk, English, coming from you."

"Listen, when I use a whore I always pay her honest and true. But raping an unwilling woman—well, I got no time for that."

"English, you're a saint."

"Well, a man's got to draw the line somewhere if'n he wants to stay true blue."

McGill's eyes glittered, looking past the moment.

"Rance, I'm here to talk about a fortune in gold, not a fat greaser bitch or a white woman gettin' screwed."

"All right, then talk away."

"You listening or are you asleep?"

"I'm listening."

"See, you and me can share it. There's enough hidden away to make us both rich men."

"You're talking about the Spanish treasure?"

"Is there any other?"

"Seems to me that Logan and the Gravedigger might have something to say about that, us splitting it two ways, I mean."

"The Gravedigger is raving mad and Logan ain't nearly as fast with the iron as he thinks he is. I can take care of both of them."

"They have a dozen men. You gonna take care of those as well?"

"If I have to."

"So, if you can do the whole thing by yourself, where do I come in?"

"You're good with a gun, Rance. I need you as an insurance policy, like."

"I don't have a gun."

McGill pulled a short-barreled Colt from his waistband and tossed it to March. "You do now."

March grabbed the gun in his right hand, jammed the muzzle between McGill's eyes, and thumbed back the hammer.

"Maybe I should just scatter your brains and keep all the gold for myself," he said.

McGill smiled. "Not with that gun, you won't. I didn't load it. The white half of me might be stupid, but the Kiowa half ain't."

March pulled the trigger.

Click!

He smiled. "Hell, I know you didn't load it. I could tell by the weight."

"So you say."

"Right. So I say."

"Well, are you in?"

"If I say no?"

"Then I'll kill you, an' no hard feelings."

"All right, I'm in. But I've got an unloaded gun and no horse."

"Hell, March," McGill said, "you want the Spanish gold handed to you on a silver platter?"

March walked alongside McGill's buckskin as they followed the Gravedigger's trail.

There was no letup in the rain, and sky was thick with clouds that looked like sooty fingerprints on gray paper.

Pretending to be weaker than he was, March stumbled often and complained that a man shouldn't be made to walk in boots with two-inch heels.

For the most part, McGill ignored him, but occasionally glanced down at him and grinned.

March's eyes studied the big breed, shrewd, calculating, and knowing.

English had said that his Kiowa half was smart, but

he'd lied about that. The Indian part was every bit as dumb as the white.

McGill's booted Winchester was on the right side of his horse, the stock pointing back, as some riders preferred.

The gunman let March walk close to the rifle, forgetting, if he ever knew, that there are some quick, confident, and sure men you don't take chances with.

Soon that ignorance would cost him his life.

Chapter 39

Three miles after leaving the canyon, McGill swung west into the Moreno Valley, then rode north across a wide grassland bordered to the east and west by tall mountains and deep forests of ponderosa pine and aspen.

"We'll head north until we sight Scully Mountain," the gunman said. "Then ride due east. We'll come up on Logan an' them by nightfall. Leastways, I will. You'll hole up somewhere until I need you."

"You know best, English," March said, pretending a humility he didn't feel.

After a while, he said,"What are you gonna do with your half of the gold, English?"

The breed laughed. "First thing, spend a week in bed with a couple of whores. After that, who knows? Probably more whores, more whiskey, and then I'll see if the cards favor me." He shook his head. "I've never been a lucky gambler, an' that's led to shootings I kinda regret."

McGill turned in the saddle and looked down at March. "How you gonna spend yours?"

He put very light emphasis on those five words, a thing March noticed. McGill didn't intend to let him live to spend half of the loot.

"I don't know, English. Improve my ranch, I guess. Maybe buy a Hereford bull."

McGill was surprised. "You're not a whorin' man?"

"I can take it or leave it. Getting too old, maybe."

"You still good with the iron? Tell me no lies, now."

"I get by."

McGill nodded. "Just as well. There can be no dead-wood on this trip."

"I'll side you, English," March said, telling a lie.

"I'll take the Gravedigger," McGill said. "Damned dead man giving orders makes my skin crawl."

"If he's already dead, how are you gonna kill him, English?"

"He'll be dead twice, is all." McGill was silent for a few moments, then said,"I've never seen him eat or drink. Damned if that's not strange."

"He buries people alive," March said. "That's what's strange."

McGill shrugged. "Hell, I don't care about him planting folks. But never drinking a drop of whiskey or a cup of coffee? Hell, Rance, that can give a feller the croup, especially a watching man like me."

But he didn't watch close enough.

Less than half a minute later English McGill was as dead as he was ever going to be.

Sure that McGill was preoccupied after his rant about the Gravedigger, March took his chance.

He reached up, yanked the Winchester from the boot, and cranked a round into the receiver even as he dived for the ground.

McGill was no pilgrim.

Quick on the draw and shoot, he palmed his Colt, the revolver coming up fast.

March's bullet hit him in the waist, an inch above the gun belt. The big .44-40 ball tore through the gunman's belly, hit a rib, and exited under his armpit.

McGill swayed in the saddle, cursed at March, and thumbed off a shot. The bullet kicked up dirt close to the older man, followed by a second that burned its way across March's thigh and drew a yelp of pain.

March fired again. The bullet thudded into McGill's chest and sudden scarlet blood flooded his mouth. March's third shot missed, but his fourth was another solid chest hit and this time McGill threw up his arms and tumbled off his horse.

Before the racketing echoes of the gunshots faded, March rose to his feet. He levered another round into the receiver, stepped around the horse's rump, and walked to McGill.

The man was still alive, his eyes wide and accusing.

"Damn it, we had a partnership," he said.

"I know, but I just dissolved it."

"Rance, you're a big son of a bitch."

"Sorry I've killed you, English, but I need your horse and your guns. I got folks to save."

"I'm shot through and through, damn you."

"I reckon you are. I got my work in pretty good."

"Hell, an' it don't hurt a bit."

English McGill's eyes closed and he died, all the life that had been in him melting into the earth with the teeming rain.

"Follow the buffalo, English," March said. "By the way, them words are for your Kiowa half. The white half can go to hell."

March reloaded McGill's Colt and stuffed it in his waistband. He did the same for the rifle, using cartridges from the gunman's belt and a box of ammunition he found in his saddlebags.

He stuffed his pockets with shells, took McGill's makings, then donned the man's slicker. He swung into the saddle and sat for a while, thinking things through.

Lester was an idiot. Mrs. Rowantree was a reformed whore who had murdered her old man. Judith was a child who looked at everything, but didn't talk. Maybe she was simple.

Using his hands as the pans of a balance scale, he put those three people in his left, his own life in the right.

He watched his hand drop on the people side, as he knew it would.

March sighed and shook his head.

"The problem is, Rance," he said aloud, "that you're too damned kind and softhearted for your own good."

Without sparing a glance for McGill, he rode into the rain.

March told himself that now, mounted and armed, he was ready, prepared to tackle anything Logan and the Gravedigger threw at him.

But he didn't believe a word of it.

Chapter 40

"I've made my decision," the Gravedigger said.

Booker said nothing, fearing what the answer to his question might be.

"I'm a merciful man," the Gravedigger said.

They were camped in a meadow beside the thin waters of Ponil Creek, the scent of wildflowers hanging in the air like a mist. The surrounding Rockies gleamed in the moonlight and there was a cool cut to the night air.

The rain had ended and the sky was full of stars.

"What have you decided?" Booker said. Relief flooded through him, but his voice was unsteady.

"They will be buried, mother and daughter, but I will bestow on them a rare privilege—later I will raise them to new life."

Booker knew he was treading on eggshells. He fought to keep his words on an even plain. "That was not our agreement. I want Mrs. Rowantree and her daughter to go free."

"I have made my decision and it is a merciful one. A noble one, Mr. Booker."

"No, it's a decision I can't accept. If you wish me to stand with you against Cass Logan, then let Mrs. Rowantree go."

The Gravedigger shook his head, slowly, almost sadly. "You push me too far, Mr. Booker," he said.

The fast movement of his arm flickered in the gloom and his taloned fingers clenched around Booker's neck. His voice was a serpent's menacing hiss. "Damn you, I'll tear your throat out."

Booker couldn't breathe. His prominent eyes popping, he grabbed the Gravedigger's hand in both of his and tried to pull it away.

His puny efforts failed, unable to match the man's incredible power.

"I'll rip you apart," the Gravedigger snarled. His fingers dug deeper and saliva ran down his chin. "You defied me."

"Leave him alone! You're killing him!"

Eliza Rowantree launched herself at the Gravedigger. Her small fists pounded on the man's shoulders as he bent his head against the blows.

Over by the fire, Logan laughed and yelled, "She's gonna whup your ass, Gravedigger."

Men laughed with him.

Eliza's woman's strength was no match for the Gravedigger's raw might, but she succeeded in saving Booker's life.

The man loosed Booker's throat and in the same motion backhanded Eliza across the face. The flat crack of knuckles hitting flesh and bone was as loud as a rifle shot.

The woman fell back and lay still. Judith ran to Eliza's side and pleaded with her to wake up.

"You," the Gravedigger said, pointing at Booker. "Don't dare defy me again."

Booker, gagging with every tormented breath, was unable to say anything. The Gravedigger's long, curved fingernails had left bloody gouges on his throat.

"Everybody come here," the Gravedigger said. "Gather around me."

Logan and a dozen other gunmen surrounded the man.

"Tomorrow I will take you to the valley where the treasure of the Spanish padres is hidden."

His words were greeted by a cheer, part enthusiastic, part derisive.

"By this time tomorrow, you'll all be rich men, burdened by all the gold you can carry," the Gravedigger said.

He waited, and got the cheer he expected, this time less mocking.

"Men, great events are about to unfold. The earth is about to give up its riches." His finger stabbed into the darkness. "To you, and you, and you, and you, Mr. Logan."

This time the sheriff led the huzzahs.

"Mr. Logan, we will need to blast the cave. Is the dynamite dry?"

"Sure is. I check it my own self every day."

"Splendid."

The Gravedigger looked around at his men. "Now,

to your blankets. Tomorrow you'll need your strength to carry . . . gold."

Another cheer and men drifted away, only to stop and watch as the Gravedigger grabbed Eliza by the hair and dragged her into a darker part of the wildflower meadow.

Judith tried to follow, but one of the gunmen held her back.

Booker struggled to his feet, a hand on his mangled throat.

"You stay right where you're at, Archibald," Logan said, grinning. "The Gravedigger don't like to be disturbed when he's at dinner."

Chapter 41

Refreshed by his sleep among the dogwoods, Ransom March rode through the night. Despite the rain, a large party of riders leaves a scar on the land and he had no difficulty following the Gravedigger's trail.

It was still dark when he passed the looming bulk of Baldy Mountain, but the rain had stopped and the peak was outlined against a backdrop of stars.

Judging by the tracks, he was close to the Gravedigger's party, and he guessed they'd camped at Ponil Creek, where there was plenty of wood, water, and graze for horses.

A coffee-drinking man, March felt the need and turned into a draw where he boiled up a brew on a hatful of fire.

He was on his second cup and third cigarette when a man's voice hailed him from the darkness.

"Hello the camp."

March grabbed the Winchester and got to his feet.

"Come in slow an' easy, like you're visiting kinfolk," he said. "I got trust in this here rifle."

"Bringing Rebecca with me, if'n that squares with you," the man said.

"Bring in whoever you please, so long as you're both downright sociable," March said.

The man loosed a hee-haw laugh. "Rebecca don't say much, mister, but she's sociable."

March heard a clanging in the gloom; then a grizzled old man leading a burro stepped into the pale glow of the firelight.

He wore greasy buckskins, a battered felt hat, and sported a gray beard that hung to his navel. He had a belted Remington around his waist, the holster slanted for a cross draw, and there was a rifle in a boot on the burro.

"Name's Benny Hinton," the old man said. "Smelled your coffee from a mile away."

"It's good and hot," March said. "Set and take a load off."

Hinton did as he was told and March sat opposite him. He kept the Winchester across his thighs, a thing the old man noticed.

"Ain't a trusting gent, are you?" he said.

"Not by nature, no." He passed Hinton a cup. "You prospecting?"

"Man and boy fer the past forty year. One time I took fifteen thousand in gold out of these mountains . . . Let me see . . . Yeah, I recollect, it were back in 'eighty-three."

March smiled. "You spend it all?"

"Every last nickel." The old man tried his coffee. "Spent it on whores, poker, and rum punches and the rest I wasted."

Hinton was silent for a few moments, then drank from his cup again. "You make good coffee, mister."

"Name's Rance March. Mister never did set right with me."

"You don't say? Would you be Ransom March the lawman that killed them Sutter brothers down McAllen way?"

"I would. They huggin' kin of your'n?"

Hinton shook his head. "Nah. I guess them boys needed killin'. They were a mean bunch." He thought for a moment. "Except maybe fer Cage. He was a Mason like me an' always struck me as true blue."

March smiled. "Cage was the son of a bitch that drew down on me first. Got some lead into me too."

"Yeah, that sounds like Cage. He was fast with the iron."

"Yeah, he could shuck a Colt's gun—that's for sure."

"Well, I'm sorry to hear that. I mean, about you getting shot, an' all."

"Came with the badge, I guess."

Hinton lit his pipe. "What brings you to this neck o' the woods, Rance?"

"Hunting a man."

"Can you give me his name? Like, he might be a friend o' mine on the scout. A man meets all kinds in these mountains."

"He's called the Gravedigger," March said.

Hinton grabbed the pipe out of his mouth to allow his chin to drop.

It took him a while to recover his composure, and

when he did, his eyes sliding from side to side, he said, "Here? He ain't close, is he?"

"I'm guessing Ponil Creek."

"Yeah, well, that's too damn close."

The old man put his pipe back in his mouth. It had gone cold but he didn't seem to notice.

"What you hunting him for, Rance? Fer buryin' folks?"

"He's holding friends of mine prisoner."

"Then forget it. They're already dead."

"Benny, that's something I got to see for myself."

"He was buried alive his own self. You know that?"

March nodded.

"He was a dead man when he went into the coffin, an' a deader man when he came out."

"Doctors make mistakes."

"His neck was broke. Hell, even a drunken pill roller can tell if a man's neck is broke."

Hinton drained his coffee cup. "I was plannin' to spread my blankets an' rest for a spell, but I'm moving on."

"I can't say as I blame you," March said.

"You should do the same, Rance. Fork that bronc and get the hell out of here. You can't kill a dead man."

"I think he's a man like any other. Crazy as a loon, but a man just the same."

"Well, you hold on to that thought."

Hinton looked at the Colt in March's waistband. "You got some spare rounds fer your iron?"

"In my pocket."

"Let me have them."

The old man opened a clasp knife and took the five shells March handed to him.

Slowly, laboriously he cut into the lead tip of each bullet and when he was done, he poured the cartridges into March's open palm.

March examined the rounds. "Hell, man, you cut an X into them."

"Yeah, I did. Only it's a Christian cross. Use them shells when you try to kill the Gravedigger."

"Benny, I ain't that superstitious."

The old man rose stiffly to his feet. "If you're goin' up against the Gravedigger, you'd better be."

March shoved the shells into his pocket. "I'll try to remember."

"I got to leave now, put a mile o' git between me and Ponil Creek," Hinton said. "Thanks fer the coffee."

"Benny, you ever meet the man?"

"The Gravedigger?"

"Yeah, him."

"I took a pot at him once with my Henry, back there in the mountains. He'd buried a friend o' mine a while afore, a poor old tin pan like me."

"Hit him?"

"I was sure I did, but he was still standin' when I lit out."

March smiled. "Were you using holy bullets?"

"God will not be mocked, Rance. Where you're going, you'll need Him on your side. Remember that."

There was no humor in Hinton. He was deadly serious and March respected that.

"I'll bear it in mind," he said.

"See you do," Hinton said, leading his burro into the new aborning day.

Chapter 42

Eliza Rowantree bathed in the creek and, like every other man in camp, Booker saw her nakedness.

She bent over, washing between her thighs, her breasts hanging between her upper arms, white, veined with blue, and tipped with coral.

Beside her, also naked, Judith played in the water, yelling, taking a child's delight in the fast-running current and darting fish.

As Booker watched, Eliza stood and splashed water on her ravaged neck, wincing as it stung. Her entire body was bruised, bitten, used hard—her neck, where the Gravedigger had fed from her, worst of all.

Booker had never seen a naked woman, had never guessed that they had a dark triangle of hair between their legs. He had always imagined they were smooth creatures, like the statues of Greek goddesses he'd seen in museums.

He had never observed Miss Lucy McIntyre, his betrothed, without garments. In fact, she had vowed that he ne'er would he see her completely naked, not even in the sacred marital bed.

"There are parts of the female body—the breasts, for example, but especially that hallowed portal lined with velvet—that can be explored, but not gazed upon. This is why we will indulge in the act of procreation, when wed, not by lamplight, but in gloom, taking no joy in the endeavor. Thus do the lady of breeding and her husband detach themselves from the brute lusts of the beasts of the field."

Booker stared at Eliza, then shook his head.

Was Miss McIntyre ashamed of her triangle?

Taking Eliza as his model, he found it didn't trouble him in the least. He quite liked it, in fact, a sign arrow pointing to the—

Booker felt a blush of shame.

Miss McIntyre would have been horrified if she knew his thoughts, and quite rightly so.

"Getting an eyeful, Archibald?"

Cass Logan stood beside Booker, a grin that was always insolent on his lips.

"No, I was just passing this way."

"Sure you were, Archie."

Logan nodded to Eliza. "Get her mounted up. We're going after the gold today."

"Let the woman and her child go, Sheriff," Booker said. "Uphold the law for a change."

Logan's grin stayed in place as his fist lashed out and hit Booker square on his receding chin.

Lying on his back, his head reeling, he looked up at

Logan. The man was standing over him, his eyes flashing anger.

"I don't need an Archibald to get uppity on me," he said.

He nodded to Eliza, who was drying herself with the tattered remains of her dress. "Do like I said and get her mounted. Both of you, and the kid."

He turned away, then stopped. "You can have her, Archie, and welcome. It's like screwing a knothole in a log."

Eliza helped Booker to his feet.

"I saw what happened," she said. "Why did he hit you?"

"He said I was uppity."

"We're moving out, aren't we?"

"Yeah. Logan wants us mounted and ready to leave."

"He thinks he'll find the treasure today?"

"That's about the size of it."

"Then this will be our last day on earth."

"Don't talk that way, Mrs. Rowantree."

"What should I do? Pray for a miracle?"

Booker had no answer.

"I've made my own miracle," Eliza said.

She looked around, then reached into the pocket of her dress.

She showed Booker the knife, a large folder with walnut panels and brass bolsters.

"I took this from the pocket of one of Logan's pigs," she said. "I'll kill Judith with it. I won't let her be buried alive."

Her gray eyes met Booker's. "If there's time, I'll kill myself."

Booker opened his mouth, but couldn't find the words to fill it. Finally he managed "Eliza . . . I'm so sorry."

"Not your fault. It's not anybody's fault but the Gravedigger's. We're trapped in an insane world, Mr. Booker, and there's no rational way out of it."

"Whom God wishes to destroy, he first makes mad," Booker said. "The Gravedigger is already marked for death."

Eliza smiled. "And who's going to kill him, Mr. Booker? You?"

"I plan to try. Today."

The woman reached up, laid her palm on Booker's cheek, and smiled like a mother humoring a dreamer child.

"Whatever you do, Mr. Booker, die well. That will be the only victory allowed you."

Chapter 43

Ransom March splashed across Ponil Creek and followed the Gravedigger's trail east.

The rain had stopped and the sky was clearing. The sun was as yet low in the sky and shadows still pooled among the peaks and valleys of the surrounding mountains. A brisk wind from the north stirred the pines and set the aspen atremble.

Once a huge bull moose with fully grown antlers crossed March's path and he reckoned the animal would dress out at nearly sixteen hundred pounds.

March rode warily, his eyes fixed on the trail ahead. If English McGill had been missed, there was a possibility riders would come looking for him.

A gunfight out in the open was no part of his plan. He needed to get the drop on Logan and them, hit hard, kill as many as he could, then skedaddle fast.

That was the plan anyway.

How he could make it work, March had no idea.

He almost rode into the Gravedigger's camp an hour after midday, but drew rein just in time.

Luckily for him, all the gunmen, Logan included, were at the other end of a U-shaped, hanging valley, rooting around the base of a rock wall overgrown with brush and scattered, wind-twisted juniper.

The woman, her daughter, and Booker stood off to one side, unguarded, an indication of Cass Logan's lack of respect for Lester as a man.

March drew into the shelter of the pines and studied the valley.

The horses were ground-tied fifty yards from him, still saddled.

He reviewed his options.

If he was one of Lester's dime novel heroes, he'd stampede the horses out of the valley, then fade into the wilderness, ready to pick off the outlaws one by one as they came searching for their mounts.

But it was a bad idea.

Some of the boys down there still had their rifles and he'd be deader than mutton a second after he started to hooraw the herd.

March's brow wrinkled in concentration. Finally he decided on a course of action: wait and see what happened.

He needed the drop, and playing Buffalo Bill and the Indians wasn't the way to give it to him.

A cheer went up from the other end of the valley.

March's long-seeing eyes scanned the distance.

Men were tearing away brush, yelling to each other, grinning.

Had they found the treasure cave?

The Gravedigger was waving his arms, yelling insanities, physically pulling men back from the rock.

When Logan and the rest paused from their labors, the Gravedigger pointed at Booker and the females and said something March couldn't hear.

Interpreting the gestures of both men, March calculated that the Gravedigger wanted to bury his prisoners before the treasure was recovered, but Logan objected.

They argued for several minutes; then the sheriff barked an order to his men.

The gunmen stepped to the pack mules, returned with shovels, and began to dig holes. They dug a bigger hole in March's belly.

The Gravedigger had forced his hand.

To March's irritation, the time to rescue the idiot, the whore, and the kid had come a lot sooner than he'd intended.

Chapter 44

March dismounted and slid his Winchester from the boot.

He dropped on his belly and crawled into the brush. The distance between him and the outlaws was at least a hundred yards, at the extreme limit of his shooting range.

Tracking his sights back and forth across the gunmen, he thought about taking a pot at the Gravedigger, who was dancing around on his peg leg as he supervised the digging men.

March almost gave up on the idea, knowing his chances of hitting the man were slight.

But finally he aimed at the Gravedigger, a jumping, arm-waving, difficult target.

Wish to hell I'd spent more time with the rifle. Gone deer huntin' maybe.

He squeezed the trigger.

A digger went down, and March cussed a blue streak.

He'd missed by at least three feet.

Levering the rifle, he looked for another target. But the gunmen, the Gravedigger included, had disappeared like ice in a summer julep.

Now probing shots were rattling through the trees above March's head, and smoke blossomed like cotton among the trees and brush at the end of the valley.

"Well, dip me in duck shit. . . ."

March lowered his rifle, his eyes wide in surprise.

Lester was making a lanky, ungainly run for it, herding the woman and her daughter in front of him.

Like Ichabod Crane chasing a butterfly, Booker ducked and pumped his arms up and down, exhorting Eliza and her daughter to run faster.

Bullets chipped rock from the canyon wall and kicked up Vs of dirt around the runners' feet. Logan and his men were getting the range.

March dusted shot after shot in the general direction of the gunmen, but hit nothing and did little to suppress their fire.

When the rifle ran dry, he opened up with his Colt, knowing full well he'd have more success throwing rocks.

But, like March, all of Logan's men were revolver fighters and lacked the skills of true riflemen.

Booker and the two females came through their barrage unhurt and March rose to his feet as they crashed into the brush near him.

"Keep going!" March yelled. "Don't stop."

On the run, Booker turned his head and said,"We thought you were dead."

"I came close," March said.

He didn't know if Booker heard him or not.

March reloaded his Colt, then the rifle.

Logan and his gunmen hadn't ventured into the open, but March fired a few shots to keep them honest.

He had to make enough of a fight to buy Booker time.

For the next five minutes March and the gunmen traded shots.

Logan and the rest still showed no inclination to rush him. Men who believe they're going to be rich by nightfall are careful with their lives.

Right now March was nothing but a pesky fly that needed to be swatted, but they preferred to swat him at a safe distance.

Cass Logan proved the truth of that.

After a lull in the firing, he yelled from the trees, "Who's out there?"

"Who wants to know?" March hollered.

"Is that you, Rance?"

"As ever was."

"But I thought you was dead."

March hammered a couple of shots in the direction of Logan's voice. "Does that convince you otherwise, Cass?"

There was a moment's pause; then Logan said, "Rance, we can talk about this. We'll cut you a share of the gold."

"How big a share?"

"Hell, I don't know how big. Equal shares for all, is what I say. I'm a man of my word, Rance, so lay down your rifle."

"What does your boss say?"

"Who?"

"Hell, you know who. The lunatic who calls himself the Gravedigger."

This time the silence stretched. Only the crickets in the long grass made any sound.

Finally, "Rance!"

"Yeah?"

"It's all settled. Lay down your gun and come out and we'll talk. You're in, Rance! In for a double share."

"Cass?"

"Yeah, Rance?"

"Share this among you."

March levered three fast shots into the trees.

"I hope you got a double share, Cass!" he yelled.

As bullets racketed through the tree branches around him, March collected his horse and eased back, putting space between him and Logan. He figured he'd outstayed his welcome.

When he reached open ground, he mounted and rode out of the valley, following Booker's tracks through the long grass.

The Gravedigger would come after them, he knew, but he reckoned that Logan and his men, intent on uncovering the Spanish gold, would stay right where they were. No doubt Logan would like to kill him, but only after the treasure was found.

March tracked Booker into a dry wash and drew

rein at the white skeleton of a juniper where he and Eliza had paused to regain their breath.

The tracks then continued along the wash and he followed. Ahead of him a dust devil performed its dervish dance, then collapsed, leaving a puff of sand to mark its passing.

There was no sound but the creak of March's saddle and the muffled footfalls of his horse. The air was still, as though the day was holding its breath, eagerly anticipating what would happen next.

The sky above the fair, far-flung land was blue from mountain peak to mountain peak, like an upturned ceramic bowl.

March lost Booker's tracks after he left the wash and rode across a stretch of flat hardpan, broken up by bunchgrass and a few stunted juniper and piñon.

After scouting his back trail and finding no evidence of a pursuit, he pushed on. He rode all the way to Ponil Creek, where he drew into cottonwoods and willow and let his horse drink.

Where the hell was Booker?

This wasn't country for a pilgrim, especially one burdened by a woman and child. Leaving aside the obvious danger of the Gravedigger and Logan, the land itself would challenge Booker, and March doubted he was man enough to handle it.

Summer or winter, the Rockies could kill you a hundred different ways and Booker would know none of them. Maybe Mrs. Rowantree had a lick of sense and could tell her butt from a watering hole, but March doubted it.

He swung out of the saddle, loosed the girth, and slid his rifle from the scabbard. Fetching his back against a shady cottonwood, he built a cigarette. Now he'd wait and see if Booker showed up, or the Gravedigger showed up, whoever came first.

Either way, he smelled trouble and hard times coming down, for himself and for others.

Chapter 45

Ransom March was alive!

The fleeting glance Booker had of him as he ran through the trees was enough to tell him that the old lawman was unhurt. Fighting fit in fact.

Behind him, he heard the hard rattle of gunfire as March tried to buck the odds, but he fought down the urge to turn back and help.

His first duty was to get Eliza and Judith out of harm's way.

The child stumbled several times, her chest wheezing, and Booker picked her up and carried her into a dry wash with a sand and pebble bottom.

"Wait, Lester," Eliza said, slowing to a walk. "I've got to rest for a spell."

She sat on the bent trunk of a skeletal juniper, her breast rising and falling as she fought for breath.

"Not long," Booker said. "I don't know how long Rance can hold them."

"That was him, wasn't it?" Eliza said. "He's alive."

"Seems like," Booker said.

"Men like him are hard to kill," Eliza said.

"Right now he's facing a dozen gunmen who would love to prove you wrong," Booker said.

He took Eliza by the elbow and helped her to her feet.

"Time to move," he said.

"Where are we headed? The canyon?"

"No, that's what the Gravedigger will expect."

"And so will Rance."

"Then let's hope Rance works it out and the Gravedigger doesn't."

Booker pointed in the direction of the tree-covered foothills opposite. "That's where we're headed. We'll hole up until dark, then try for the canyon. We can cross at first light."

"Logan and the Gravedigger could be waiting for us," Eliza said.

"Maybe, but I think Logan has more on his mind. He wants the Spanish treasure."

"Then let's go," Eliza said.

Behind them, as Booker led the way across a stretch of flat rock, there was a pause in the firing from the valley.

But by the time they reached the foothills, there was still no sign of March.

A narrow arroyo, overgrown with brush and cactus, looked promising.

Booker led the way inside and was pleased when the gulch opened up into a grassy area about an acre in extent. From somewhere close he heard the splash of falling water.

"It's not great, but it will have to do," he said.

"Lester," Eliza said, "I hope you know what the hell you're doing."

"So do I, Mrs. Rowantree," Booker said. "So do I."

Chapter 46

"The hell with Archibald and the woman," Cass Logan said. "We can kill them later. Right now I want to uncover the gold before dark."

"You can," the Gravedigger said. "It's right there waiting, behind the rock fall."

Logan lifted his eyes to the canyon wall looming above the cave.

"Damn it, there's still a pile of rock up there," he said. "If we use dynamite we'll bring it down on top of us."

"Then start digging, Cass. A dozen men can move that rubble quickly."

A limestone ledge above the cave had caught and held a pyramid of massive boulders that had tumbled down from the mountain slope the last time someone used dynamite to seal the cave mouth.

The pile looked safe, but appearances were deceiving, as Logan well knew. Any kind of vibration could dislodge the whole damn thing and crush the life out of anyone standing under it.

As though reading his thoughts, the Gravedigger said,

"Slow and steady wins the race, Cass. Just tell your men to be careful."

Logan looked at the boulders again, an ominous, threatening mass at least forty feet wide and twice that high, some of the rocks the size of log cabins.

"Damn, that scares me," he said. "Who the hell used dynamite the last time?"

"I did," the Gravedigger said. "To keep the treasure safe."

"Hell, why didn't you just take the gold with you?"

"I was alone. I couldn't carry it all. But now I've returned for it."

"You mean for your share," Logan said.

"Of course, Cass. I want no more than my due."

Logan studied the blocked cave entrance again. "Damn, dynamite would have made this job so much easier."

"Treasure hunting is not for the fainthearted, Cass," the Gravedigger said. His yellow skin stretched tight to his skull.

Logan smiled. He yelled to his men to get away from the entrance to the cave, then turned to the Gravedigger again. "Split ass over there and lift out the first rock."

"Are you trying to scare me, Cass?"

"You ain't fainthearted, are you?"

"What's it like, Cass?"

"What the hell are you talking about?"

"To be buried alive. What's it like?"

"How would I know?"

"The man March shot was alive when I buried him. What's it like?"

Logan's gun came up fast. "You're loco. Now git over there and start pulling down them damned rocks."

The Gravedigger gave no sign that he'd heard or even noticed the gun. His eyes were as black and dead as coal.

"What do the worms do? Do they wiggle and wriggle and jiggle and lay eggs in your ears and mouth? What's it like, Cass? Tell me."

"Mister, you'll find out the answers to that real soon if you don't get over to the cave and start lifting rocks. I swear, I'll blow your damned fool head off."

"You don't know the answer, Cass, do you? But you will. Oh, you will."

The triple click of the Colt hammer was loud in the silence.

The Gravedigger smiled. "You can't kill me, Cass. I died already."

"Try me."

"Maybe the gold isn't there. Maybe I lied. Maybe it's somewhere else."

Logan scowled, not liking it. "Damn you, is the gold in the cave?"

"Pull down the rubble, Cass. See for yourself."

The sheriff wanted to kill the Gravedigger real bad. But if the man lied and the gold was hidden elsewhere, he'd never find it.

He lowered the hammer of his Colt and slid it into the holster.

"One day I'll kill you," he said.

"But not today, Cass," the Gravedigger said. "Not today."

Logan ignored the man and yelled, "You men, clear the cave mouth and let's get it done. Move slow and careful."

"You gonna be with us, Cass?" a man said.

"What's wrong, Luke? Scared a rock will fall on your head?"

"Something like that."

"All right, come with me. I'll hold your hand."

Men laughed, then followed Logan to the cave.

The Gravedigger watched them go, a satisfied smile twitching at his lips.

Chapter 47

They were recaptured, lost, or dead; there was no fourth possibility.

Ransom March got to his feet, shaking his head.

It didn't surprise him any; neither of them had the sense to pour rainwater out of a boot.

He'd planned to wait until nightfall if necessary to see if they showed up. But March wasn't long on patience, and waiting didn't come easily to him.

He stepped to his horse and took out a strip of antelope jerky from McGill's saddlebags and chewed, thinking. The meat, poorly prepared, was tough, salty, and gamy but helped fill a hole.

By the time he drank from his canteen to wash away the taste, March had made up his mind.

He'd go looking for them.

"And damned if I know why," he said.

The buckskin tossed its head but didn't seem to care one way or the other.

It is the habit of men who ride long trails to talk to themselves, and March did. But his conversation was limited to a stream of profane invective directed at Lester Booker.

If he'd allowed himself to get taken again, March was in a mind to let the Gravedigger bury him. The world would never miss one more big city idiot.

But then he thought of the child, and knew he couldn't stand by and let the Gravedigger kill her horribly.

"Damn world would be a fine place if there was no stupid people in it," March said.

He rode away from the canyon and back in the direction he'd come.

The badly smoked jerky festering in his stomach began to give him gas, and his mood rapidly went from bad to worse to much worse.

Scouting the ground as he rode, March went all the way to the stretch of hardpan before he drew rein in the shelter of some aspen. He looked around and saw no movement but the wind in the trees.

He briefly thought about calling out for Lester, but dismissed the idea. Making all that noise could bring Logan and the rest down on him pretty quick.

March studied the serried foothills west of the hardpan.

Now, where would an idiot choose to hide?

An arroyo probably, and a box at that.

Gas blew bubbles in March's belly, pressing his swollen gut against the gun in his waistband. His irritation grew.

"I swear, Lester," he said aloud, "I'm gonna kick your skinny ass. Why didn't you head for the canyon?"

The question hung in the air without an answer.

March kneed the buckskin out of the aspen and rode down a slight incline to the flat rock.

There was no sign of Logan and his gunmen, a fact that didn't surprise him. By now they'd uncovered the treasure and were busy splitting the spoils.

March smiled slightly at the idea of holy objects being squabbled over by an unholy crowd.

He rode toward the foothills, his rifle across the saddle horn, his eyes scanning the forested terrain ahead of him.

A minute later the skin on his back crawled, instinct warning him what was coming.

Knowing he wasn't going to make it in time, he swung the buckskin around and started to bring up the Winchester.

He caught a fleeting glimpse of what was behind him before his world collapsed into darkness.

The Gravedigger . . . rifle to his shoulder . . . a puff of smoke . . . a noise like thunder . . .

March felt a club hit him just above the left ear. The Winchester spun from his hands, and the suddenly vertical hardpan rushed to meet him.

Damn, the lunatic can shoot.

That final thought before he plummeted into the abyss. . . .

Chapter 48

Lester Booker jumped when he heard the shot.

"March?" Eliza said. Her eyes were frightened.

"I don't know. Stay here."

Booker rose to his feet and walked along the arroyo to its mouth. What he saw drove him to take cover behind a stand of prickly pear.

The Gravedigger stood over March's still body, a Winchester rifle in his hands. The man was smiling, a skeletal grimace.

Then, in a display of enormous strength, he lifted March and threw him across the buckskin.

The Gravedigger looked around, picked up March's rifle, and led the horse across the hardpan toward the hanging valley.

Impotent rage built up inside Booker. He had no gun, no guts, a powerless bystander to tragedy.

"Is it March?"

Eliza kneeled beside him, her eyes on the buckskin and its burden.

"The Gravedigger shot him."

"Is he dead?"

"I don't know."

Booker looked at the woman, pain in his eyes. "I couldn't help him."

"No, you couldn't."

"No gun, no guts," Booker said, giving voice to his thoughts.

"An unarmed man doesn't run into a rifle. What could you have done?"

"I don't know."

"We'll go for help. We can leave now, cross the canyon well before dark, and head west. We're bound to find a settlement with a lawman."

"We have no canteen and no food. We could die out there."

This was from Judith, the first coherent words Booker had ever heard her say.

The girl surprised him. "She's right," he said. "We could get lost and wander around the mountains for days, weeks maybe, and then die."

"Then what do you suggest?" Eliza said.

"I want you and Judith to remain here where there's water."

"And you?"

"I'm going after Rance."

Eliza shook her head. "You're crazy. What can you do?"

"I don't know."

The woman placed her hand on Booker's shoulder. "Lester, you're not one of those frontier heroes you want to write your stupid stories about. You're a city slicker and you don't know squat about anything."

Booker forced a smile. "Mrs. Rowantree, you're right. I'm not a Prince of the Plains. But neither is Rance. He's just an ordinary man who bites the bullet and does what he has to do."

He looked into Eliza's troubled eyes. "That takes a special kind of courage, like the way he came back here looking for us."

Scorn touched the woman's voice. "Seems like you've changed your mind about Ransom March pretty quick."

Now Booker's smile was genuine. "I've grown up pretty quick on this trip."

Eliza shook her head. "No, you haven't. But maybe you've made a start. A small start."

"Whatever you say, Mrs. Rowantree."

A silence stretched; then Eliza reached into her pocket. She held out the knife she'd taken from Logan's gunman. "It's not much, but it might help."

Booker took the knife. "Don't move until I get back," he said.

The woman didn't answer, and he said it again.

"We'll stay here until this time tomorrow. Then we'll walk on out. There's water at the bottom of Ponil Canyon and it might see us through."

"And fish," Booker said. "Maybe you could catch a fish."

It was meant to be a lame joke, but Eliza took it seriously.

"Maybe I can," she said.

"I'm going," Booker said. He rose to his feet, a tall, skinny man with no chin. He looked at the woman. "Mrs. Rowantree, if we don't meet again, I want you to know that I'm sorry for all the things that happened to you."

"I'm sorry too, Lester. Sorry I had to kill my husband. Sorry that Judith had no childhood. Sorry that I was raped. Sorry for March. Sorry for you. Sorry for myself." Her eyes met Booker's and held. "But looking back in sorrow don't pay the fiddler to play at the ball. Me, Judith, we have to keep on going, keep on living."

"You're a woman of courage, Mrs. Rowantree," Booker said.

She shook her head. "No, I'm not. You said it yourself when you talked about Ransom March. Like him, I'm just an ordinary human being who's biting the bullet and doing what she has to do. And like it did March, life taught me that lesson the hard way."

"Mrs. Rowantree, I—"

"Please, Lester, I don't want to talk anymore. Just . . . just go do what you have to do."

Booker saw by her empty eyes that the woman's talking was done.

He nodded to her, then stepped out of the arroyo.

"Lester," she called out after him, "no matter what happens, when you return to New York you can hold your head high in the company of men."

Booker did not answer.

He had a lump in his throat the size of a green apple.

Chapter 49

"You killed one of my men, Mr. March," the Gravedigger said. "No great loss, I admit, but irritating nonetheless."

"You go to hell," March said.

He had a pounding headache, the legacy of the bullet that had grazed him, and his left elbow was bruised and swollen from his fall onto the hardpan.

The Gravedigger smiled. "I like you, Mr. March. You've got sand. One day I'll raise you to glory, never fear."

March looked into the man's eyes, ablaze with the fever of his madness. "You damned lunatic, you've buried so many people over the years I bet you can't even remember where you planted half of them."

"Ah, but I can. Every single one." He leaned closer to March, talking into his face. "I'll remember where you are buried, dear friend. Don't concern yourself about that."

The Gravedigger waited, but March said nothing.

"But all that is for later," the Gravedigger said, filling in the silence. "Perhaps tonight, after the men have had supper."

He'd been squatting on his haunches and now he

got to his feet. He extended a hand to March. "Come, I have something to show you. I believe it will amuse, and perhaps titillate, you."

March ignored the man's hand and struggled upright. His head ached, as though a blacksmith were using his skull as an anvil.

The Gravedigger grinned. "My bullet went where it was aimed. I didn't try to kill you, Mr. March."

March lifted his fingers to his scalp. He felt crusted blood.

Angry now, he said,"You're a damned liar. Nobody shoots that good."

The Gravedigger's expression didn't change. "I do," he said. "And after I raise you up, so will you. We will conquer the world, Mr. March."

"Just me and you, huh?"

"No, our army will number in the thousands."

"All the people you plan to bury?"

"Yes, I will lead a victorious army of the dead, obedient, unquestioning, slaves to my will."

"Mister, you're crazy and your shadow has fallen on the ground for too long," March said. "I've never met a man who needs killing as much as you."

"And I've never met a man as contrary as you, Mr. March. You argue about everything. If I say black, you say white. It's all becoming very tiresome."

The Gravedigger stood in the dappled shade of the trees, a creature of light and shadow, as though parts of his body had started to rot. "Now come with me. I want you to see that part of the Spanish treasure already unearthed."

"Do I have a choice?"

"None."

"Then lead the way."

The recurring fever of the Gravedigger's insanity once again transformed the man's face into a grinning skull.

"What's it like, Mr. March?"

"Lay that out for me."

"To lie in the grave. Alive. Alone. Waiting. Listening. What's it like?"

"I don't know."

"It turned my hair white. Did the terror of being buried alive with the worms drive me to insanity?"

"Yup, I reckon it did."

"No, it didn't. I'm as sane as you. Saner, perhaps. The conqueror worm failed to make of me a fool."

The Gravedigger closed his eyes and intoned in the hollow voice of a dead man,

But see, amid the mimic route.
A crawling shape intrude.
A bloodred thing that writhes from out
The scenic solitude!
It writhes!—it writhes!—with mortal pangs
The mimes become its food,
And seraphs sob at vermin fangs,
In human gore imbued.

"Do you know who wrote that, Mr. March?" the Gravedigger said.

"You?"

"No, it was penned by Mr. Edgar Allan Poe. He talks

of the conqueror worm, and well he should. The worms devoured his brain and drove him to madness."

The Gravedigger peered into March's face. "Did he know what it was like?"

"Maybe. He sounds near as crazy as you," March said.

"How dare you! He did not know! Poe was a charlatan. He never lay alive in the coffin, in the crawling, heaving grave."

"My mistake," March said.

He looked around, searching for a way to make a break. There was none. Logan and his men were so close, near the base of the valley wall, he could hear their voices. They'd gun him before he covered ten yards.

The crimson light faded from the Gravedigger's eyes. "Well, we will speak no more of Mr. Poe. One day, perhaps I'll find where he lies and resurrect him to life. But then, I may not."

He smiled. "Now, Mr. March, my friend, let us see the treasure."

"Mister, I ain't your friend," March said.

"After you lie in the grave for a while, possibly years, you'll change your mind."

It dawned on Ransom March then that the only hope he had of getting out of this alive was Lester—wherever the hell he was.

Lester . . . his rescuer.

He knew then, with a terrible certainty, that he was a dead man.

Chapter 50

Booker entered the valley and took refuge in the trees where March had made his fight with Logan and his men.

The sun hung low in the sky, and shadows had formed among the trees and angled along the base of the ledges and fissures along the rock walls.

Near Booker, in a patch of wildflowers, late-working bees hummed among the blossoms, ignoring him as they went about their business.

The sky was pale blue, free of cloud.

Laughter and shouts of men rose from the opposite end of the valley, but Booker saw no one. As he'd suspected for a while now, he badly needed spectacles, both for reading and distance, which wasn't surprising.

Poor sight was a distinguishing feature of the Booker family, and his mother had worn glasses since she was fourteen. Though not yet kin, his betrothed, Miss Lucy McIntyre, had also donned spectacles at an early age, quite thick ones at that, though they did have the advantage of making her rather prominent blue eyes look huge.

Booker decided not to dwell on the fair, far faces of his loved ones.

All his attention must now be focused on freeing Rance.

If the Gravedigger decided not to bury him tonight, then he could be freed. If, on the other hand, his interment was scheduled for earlier, it would fall to Booker to attempt a daring rescue.

He licked suddenly dry lips. It would take a famed pistoleer, a Prince of the Plains, to accomplish such a feat. Booker knew he was neither.

For a moment he grasped the knife in his pocket, and was comforted by the solid feel of iron and wood. He doubted that he could thrust the blade into a man, but it would cut rope if Rance was bound hand and foot.

But that would have to wait until dark.

Booker needed no reminder that he was tall and ungainly, not in the least athletic, more of a bookworm, but somehow he'd need to creep about in darkness like an Indian and not be seen.

The prospect worried him. Worse, it scared him.

But he had it to do. There was no one else.

His thoughts went to Mrs. Rowantree and Judith. How were they faring? They had a water source, but that was all. He did not fear that the woman would be discovered by Logan's men—they were all here—but there was always the danger of wild beasts, wolves and bears and moose and the like.

Thank God the wild Indians were all gone. That was a blessing.

Booker closed his eyes, drowsed as the bees hummed a lullaby. He heard distant voices, Logan's men horsing around. Crickets chirped in the grass . . . the wind whispered through the tree branches . . .

His breathing slowed, his shoulders warmed by splashing sunlight.

He slept. . . .

Chapter 51

Eliza Rowantree saw the rider when he was still a ways off, a black man riding a mouse-colored pony.

She grabbed Judith's hand and pulled her deeper into the arroyo.

"What's wrong, Ma?" the girl asked.

"Rider coming. He could be one of Logan's men."

Judith caught her mother's urgency and said nothing as Eliza led her into a clump of bushes at the base of the arroyo wall.

It was not much of a hiding place, but the woman prayed that it would not be needed. Hopefully the man would keep on going and ride past.

He didn't.

A few agonizing minutes ticked past; then the man rode into the clearing.

He was a tall black man with wide shoulders, handsome enough with iron gray hair showing under his battered army campaign hat. He wore a Colt on his waist, and a rifle was booted under his right knee.

The man kneed his grulla forward until he was only a few yards from the bushes.

"Beggin' your pardon, ma'am. I'm seeking a man named Ransom March," the rider said. "Have you seen him by any chance?"

Eliza made no answer. She put a forefinger to her lips, warning Judith to be silent.

"I can see by the way the mesquite bush is trembling that you're afraid," the rider said, this time with a hint of amusement. "There's no need to be. My name is Lafe Stringfellow and I work at Mr. March's ranch."

If the man wanted to kill her, he could.

Eliza stepped out of the bush, holding Judith's hand in hers.

Lafe touched his hat. "Pleased to meet you, ma'am. I'm afraid you have the advantage of me."

"Eliza Rowantree. This here is my daughter, Judith."

Again Lafe touched his hat. "Charmed, ladies, I'm sure."

In an odd way, the man's old-world courtesy reassured Eliza. She said, "Why are you hunting Mr. March?"

"To take him home. He will wander off when I'm not there to keep an eye on him."

"Step down," Eliza said. "But I'm afraid I've nothing to offer you."

"I can take care of that," Lafe said. "I've got both coffee and grub."

"We'd be grateful for both," Eliza said, hunger driving her beyond politeness.

"Figured that." Lafe grinned.

* * *

"Tracked the boss all the way from the Black Mesa country," Lafe said, watching Eliza drink coffee, pleased that she enjoyed it so.

"How did you track him this far?" Eliza said.

"When Rance March is on a manhunt, he tends to leave dead men behind him. There's that. And then there's the fact that I fit Apaches for a spell and they taught me how to follow a trail, and a few other things besides."

Lafe laid bacon on a slice of sourdough bread that showed specks of green. He passed the food to Judith. "Eat, little darlin'. You still look sharp set."

His eyes went to Eliza again. "Near as I can tell, Rance is shadowing at least a dozen riders. The Gravedigger and his men."

"And a renegade sheriff by the name of Cass Logan," Eliza said.

Something in the woman's eyes gave Lafe pause. "Here, Rance isn't dead, is he?"

"Not yet."

"Where is he, ma'am?"

"In a canyon across the hardpan."

Sparing only mention of her rape and the killing of her husband, Eliza told Lafe about the events leading up to Ransom's capture.

When she finished, the man said, "And Archibald went to find him?"

"Lester."

"Archibald, Lester—God help us and Rance either way."

"Yes, he went to find him. He left just before you got here."

"Boy's got more sand than I figured," Lafe said.

"They'll kill him. Logan and his men."

"Uh-huh. I'd say you can bet the farm on that."

"What are you going to do, Mr. Stringfellow?"

"I'm studying on it, ma'am."

"There're too many of them."

"I know that, ma'am."

After a silence, Lafe said,"From what you've told me, nobody's yet taken the war to the Gravedigger."

"Mr. March did. He did some shooting, remember, when he helped us escape."

"How many did he kill?"

"I don't know. I think he hit one man."

"I bet he was aiming at somebody else. Boss can't shoot worth a damn unless he's close enough to raise a blister."

"What are you going to do?"

"You asked me that already, ma'am."

"Yes, I did, didn't I?"

Lafe smiled. "And I'm still studying on it, ma'am."

He didn't think on it long.

Getting to his feet, Lafe said,"You stay right where you're at, ma'am. I'll be back."

Eliza looked alarmed. "What are you going to do?"

"Rescue Archibald, then take the fight to the Gravedigger, give him something else to think of besides burying folks."

"Please, Mr. Stringfellow, be careful."

"I plan to, ma'am, and I hope I'm not too late. I want Mr. March alive—not six feet under."

Chapter 52

"Damn it, is he still alive?"

"Mr. Logan, please, Mr. March is our guest," the Gravedigger said.

"I say we kill him now," Logan said. "He's becoming a damned nuisance."

"Mr. March will be disposed of in due course. But it will be my way, Mr. Logan, not yours."

He looked at March. "Ah, I see you're impressed."

"Hell, that's a pile of gold," March said.

"How much, Mr. Logan?" the Gravedigger said.

"Near as I can figure, close to a hundred pounds when it's melted down."

Chalices, plates, candlesticks, and jugs lay in a gleaming heap, all of exquisite workmanship.

"This stuff came from Spain," the Gravedigger said. "It's too finely crafted to be of native origin."

March looked at the sweaty men clustered around Logan and did a fast calculation in his head.

"Cass, a hundred pounds of gold at twenty-one dollars

an ounce, divided among a dozen men, is only twenty-eight hundred dollars each. What's that? Enough to keep a man in whores and whiskey for a six-month, if he's real careful and counts every penny?"

March grinned. "To make a decent profit, Logan, you're gonna have to get rid of most of these boys."

"You shut your trap or I'll shut it for you," Logan said, his eyes blazing.

But March had struck a nerve.

Suddenly the gunmen around Logan exchanged glances, and he heard a few discontented murmurs. Most hadn't even known what a pound of gold was worth before now.

The Gravedigger and Logan had promised to make them rich, but March had nailed that lie to the counter.

"There's no need for panic, gentlemen," the Gravedigger said, smiling, confident, a man about to save the day.

"What you have found are worthless baubles. The real treasure lies deeper within the cave, silver and gold coin, enough to fill a dozen wagons."

Logan, unshaven, dirty, his nerves stretched taut, snorted his disbelief. "We've been all over the damned cave," he said. "This is the only gold we found."

"Ah, but did you dig?"

"What the hell are you talking about?"

"The coin is buried deep."

"Then let's get at it," Logan said.

The men around him regained their enthusiasm and a few grabbed shovels.

"Not so fast," the Gravedigger said. "The coin is buried in the darkest part of the cave. You'll need to make torches."

March grinned. "He's stalling, Logan. Can't you tell? There is no more gold."

The sheriff looked at the Gravedigger, shades of doubt in his eyes. "Are you lying to me? If you are—"

"The gold is there, Mr. Logan. But you must have light to dig for it. Remember, you must go carefully or the whole mountain could fall on top of you."

The Gravedigger turned to March. "You disappoint me, Mr. March. So much so that I no longer wish you to be a part of my enterprise. I will not tolerate your disloyalty and treachery a moment longer."

He nodded to Logan. "Shoot him."

Chapter 53

Keeping to shadow, Lafe Stringfellow rode into the hanging valley and dismounted when he reached the trees.

He went to a knee and, a long-seeing man, he scanned the terrain in front of him. A few men stood near the north rock wall, but he lost them when they walked back into the shelter of trees.

Lafe nodded, his face grim. That must be where the treasure cave was located, and probably where Rance was held.

He froze, startled by a noise to his left, a guttural animal grunt.

Lafe cursed under his breath. He wasn't yet ready to carry out his planned attack, and the last thing he needed was a wild pig kicking up a fuss and drawing attention to his hiding place.

He laid his Sharps on the grass at his feet, and drew a foot-long bowie knife from his boot.

He'd deal with the pig, and then the Gravedigger.

Crouching low, Lafe glided like a ghost through the

underbrush. He barely moved the bushes and made no sound.

The grunting was louder now, just ahead of him.

Gradually the underbrush cleared, giving way to a small clearing, dappled with shade from the surrounding pines.

Lafe's face twisted into a scowl. It was not a wild pig. It was . . .

Lester.

The man lay with his head against a tree trunk, plug hat tipped over his eyes, mouth wide-open, snoring.

Lafe kneeled beside him and placed the edge of the bowie against the sleeping man's throat. He pressed harder.

Booker woke with a start.

"Archibald, if I'd been one of Logan's men . . . you're dead."

Booker tried to talk, his eyes fixed on the blade at his neck. He failed, tried again.

"I . . . I didn't plan to move until dark," he said finally.

"And in the meantime you planned on sleeping away the day snoring like a pig?"

"I . . . I must have dropped off. . . ."

"Archibald," Lafe said, "I've a mind to kill you myself, but I don't have time."

He rose to his feet and slid the knife back into his boot. "Get back to the arroyo. Mrs. Rowantree has coffee."

"What are you going to do?"

"Stir things up some."

"Take me with you."

"Hell no, Archibald. You'd fall asleep."

Lafe retrieved his Sharps, then made his way back to the grulla and swung into the saddle.

"You're going to hear some shooting, Archibald," he said as Booker joined him. "Don't let it skeer you none."

"The name's Lester—Mr. Booker to you—and I don't scare that easily."

Lafe shrugged. "Just as you say, Archibald."

Booker watched him ride through the trees and into the open.

The big black man advanced until he was halfway to the end of the valley, then drew rein. He booted the Sharps, then slid his long-barreled Colt from the leather.

Lafe took off his hat, wiped the band with his fingers, and settled it on his head again. He turned his face to the sky and remained that way for a long time before looking to his front again.

To Booker, these seemed like nervous gestures, but when made by a man like Lafe Stringfellow, there was no telling for sure.

It rankled that the man had passed judgment on him.

But then a voice whispered in his head, *Lester, it's your own damned fault.*

It angered him that he knew it was.

Sleeping on guard duty was a serious offense, and he believed soldiers could still be hanged for it.

It had been his own self-loathing and chagrin talking when he'd told Lafe to call him Mr. Booker. But he'd turned it outward, deflected it from himself, and directed it at Lafe, along with the implication that he, as a white man, merited respect from a Negro.

But he'd given Lafe no reason to respect him, as any kind of man, and inside Booker the knife twisted deeper.

He turned away. Lafe was right. He'd go have coffee and cake with the ladies.

Booker stopped in his tracks as a bloodcurdling yell splintered the air behind him.

He swung around, in time to see Lafe charging, screaming a war cry that was half Apache, half Rebel yell, and all terrifying.

Despite himself, Booker grinned, waved his hat, jumped up and down, and added his own huzzahs to Lafe's wild cries.

Then he charged after the big man, waving the open folding knife like a saber.

Chapter 54

Cass Logan thumbed back the hammer of his Colt and grinned. "Sweet dreams, Rance."

"You go to hell," March said.

Logan, his taunting not yet done, opened his mouth to speak, then snapped it shut as another bloodcurdling cry echoed through the valley.

A moment later death came calling on the gunmen around the entrance to the cave.

Suddenly Lafe Stringfellow was among them like a black avenging angel.

The Colt in his right hand bucked as he fired shot after shot into the scattering gunmen. One man went down, then another.

Logan, steadier than the rest, tried to bring his gun to bear. March dived at him and brought him to the ground. Logan instinctively jerked the trigger, trying for the older man's belly, but his shot went wide.

Logan was bigger, stronger, and younger than March, but a rock is a great equalizer. As the two men struggled, March reached out, grabbed the rock, and slammed it into the side of Logan's head.

The sheriff groaned, then lay still.

March grabbed Logan's gun and sprang to his feet. He turned, looking for Lafe, but the big man's shooting was over and he'd already lit out.

Logan's men had recovered their wits and were firing. Bullets kicked up dirt around March and split the air close to his head.

He ran for the cave, felt a bullet slam into him, but kept going. Then he was inside, lurching through dank darkness that smelled of bat shit and the odor of ancient padres preserved in limestone rock.

Lafe hammered across the open toward the entrance to the valley.

Lester saw him, turned, and ran in the opposite direction.

Without checking his horse, Lafe swung to his right, grabbed the back of Lester's coat in his blacksmith's hand, and lifted him off the ground.

He didn't let go of his kicking, yelling burden, until they were clattering across the hardpan and the valley lay behind them.

March found a dogleg in the cave that offered cover, but allowed him to keep the entrance in sight.

He was not alone.

Opposite lay the skeleton of a man, scraps of leather and tattered cloth still clinging to his yellow bones. As his eyes grew accustomed to the darkness, he saw several more, including two close together, one with its bony arm across the shoulder of the other. They'd died that way, one trying to comfort his companion as their death approached.

March figured these were the remains of the men who had accompanied the Gravedigger on his last expedition to the cave. They'd been hit by a rock fall and entombed.

March doubted that the landslide had been an act of God. More likely the act of a madman using dynamite.

"Mr. March, do you hear me?"

The Gravedigger's voice.

"I hear you, and be damned to ye for a raving lunatic," March said.

"I don't want to hurt you, Mr. March. I spoke in haste and anger before. Step out and let's be perfect friends again."

"Go to hell."

It was coming, and March prepared himself. He checked the loads in the Colt. Four rounds left, as he'd expected. The range was short, but four shots did nothing to reassure a man.

He grimaced from pain as he moved, bringing his gun to bear on the cave entrance.

Then they came for him.

Six gunmen charged into the cave, jostling each other for gun room. March cut loose, firing fast.

He thumbed the Colt dry. Only four rounds, but it was enough.

As the smoke drifted, two men lay dead on the cave floor. The rest had scampered without firing a shot.

"Hey, Cass," March yelled, "how did that set with ya, huh?"

"You bastard, Rance. You broke my damned head."

"Nah, I didn't. Your damned head is too thick."

March scuttled to the dead men, grabbed their cartridge belts, and returned to cover.

The exertion tired him, but did not come as a surprise.

Experience had taught him that he was hit hard. A dying man.

Chapter 55

"I think I saw Rance run into the cave, but I'm not sure. Things were happening fast." Lafe Stringfellow drank from his coffee, steam clouding his face. "But I think I did."

"How do we get him out of there?" Booker said.

"I don't know. Maybe we can't."

"You mean you'll just ride away?"

"I mean, maybe we can't."

Booker was silent, thinking. Then he said, "I wasn't much help, was I?"

"Not much."

"You tried, Lester," Eliza said. "Nobody can fault you."

"A man tries, but maybe he don't try hard enough," Lafe said.

"For goodness' sake, all he had was a folding knife," Eliza said. "What was he supposed to do?"

"The man asked me if he was any help, ma'am," Lafe said. "I told him."

The night crowded close, kept at bay by a small fire

that guttered and cracked in the wind. Coyotes were
hunting rodents nearby, their cries loud in the darkness.

"Maybe we can bargain with them," Eliza said.

"With what?" Lafe said.

"Tell them if they give us Rance we'll ride away and
leave them alone."

Lafe smiled. "Ma'am, I don't think they're afraid of
us."

"I wish my betrothed was here," Booker said. "She
always seems to know what to do in a crisis."

"Is she pretty?" A woman's question from Eliza coming out of the blue. Beside her, Judith seemed to eagerly anticipate Booker's answer.

"I've never really thought about it. I suppose she is,
in a way."

"In what way?" Lafe said. He sounded sour.

"She has a trim figure," Booker said.

"Corsets," Lafe said.

"And her hair is thick and lustrous."

"A wig," Lafe said.

"Her teeth are white, though a little prominent. Her
front teeth, I mean."

"So she's as bucktoothed as a beaver, huh?" Lafe
said.

"Mr. Stringfellow, I know you're cross with me for
not helping more in the valley, but that's no excuse
to criticize the woman I intend to wed," Booker said.
"She's a lady of superior deportment and fine breeding. She excels in needlework, the harpsichord, and can

quote chapter and verse from the works of the Brontë sisters."

"No offense, Archibald. I was just trying to get a picture of the gal in my mind, was all." Lafe sipped his coffee. "What's her name?"

"Miss Lucy McIntyre."

"A pretty name," Eliza said. Judith nodded.

"If Miss Lucy was here, what would her advice be?" Lafe said.

"I don't know," Booker said. "I'd have to ask her."

"Well, she ain't here, so we have to work it out for ourselves," Lafe said.

He rose to his feet. "I'm going back to the valley. Maybe there's another way into that cave."

"No, Mr. Stringfellow, you'll get killed," Eliza said.

"Ma'am, Rance March is my boss and I ride for the brand. I got it to do."

"I'll come with you," Booker said, rising.

Lafe opened his mouth to speak, but never got a chance to form the words.

"Boy," a voice from the darkness said, "stay right where you're at or I'll drop you fer sure."

Lafe thought about it.

He was good with the iron, fast and sure on the draw and shoot. But when five men carrying rifles and scatterguns stepped into the circle of the firelight, he bowed to the inevitable and made pretend he was a statue.

"Smart fer a black man, ain't you?" Cass Logan said.

Chapter 56

"Hell, you wasn't hard to find," Logan said. "Smelled your smoke from way off." He shook his head in pretend disbelief. "Dumbest bunch of pilgrims I ever did meet."

"What do you want with us, Logan?" Booker asked. His fists were clenched at his sides, and his chin would have jutted if he'd had a chin to jut.

"Well," Logan said, "normally I'd say because the Gravedigger wants to bury you, on account of how he's tetched in the head. But that ain't the reason."

"Then what is the reason? And damn you fer a yellow-bellied skunk," Lafe said.

"The reason"—Logan stepped quickly to Lafe and clubbed him across the head with the stock of his rifle—"is that you're bargaining chips."

Lafe lay on the ground, the left side of his head bloody.

Logan looked at him. "I don't take lip from a black man. Never have and never will."

"Don't say anything, Mr. Stringfellow," Eliza said.

"He'll kill you." She rushed to Lafe and kneeled beside him. She took his head in her lap and looked up at Logan. "You want to strike a bargain with the Grave-digger?"

"Hell no. Rance March is holed up in a cave and he's keeping me away from a fortune in gold and silver. He may be hit, maybe not, but I don't have the time or patience to starve him out."

"If he comes out, you'll spare our lives," Eliza said.

"Something like that. But I want him the hell away from there. He's already killed two of my men and . . ."

Logan's voice trailed away and he looked stricken. "Oh, hell . . ."

"What gives, Cass?" a man said.

"Is the dynamite still in the cave?" Logan asked him.

"Yeah. You said to store it there away from the rain."

"So what's the problem, Cass?" another man asked.

"The problem, you idiot, is that March has a case of dynamite. He could bring down the whole damned mountain and bury the cave forever."

"With him in it?" the man said. "That ain't likely."

"It ain't likely if he isn't hit bad," Logan said. "If he's got a bullet in his belly and figures he's gonna cash in anyhow, he just might blow up the cave, and us with it."

"Then best we get to cussin' and discussin', Cass," the man said. "Get these folks over there."

"All but him," Logan said, nodding to Lafe. "I've always enjoyed killing a man before supper."

"Kill Lafe, and you'll be making a big mistake," Booker said.

"How come, Archibald?"

"I don't think Rance will come out of the cave for Mrs. Rowantree and me. But Lafe is his hired hand and he sets store by him."

Logan looked at Lafe. "Is that true?"

"Yeah," Lafe said, "I work for him."

Logan nodded. "Count yourself fortunate. Get on your feet."

"I don't reckon he'll come out for me either," Lafe said.

"Then you'll be one shit-out-of-luck feller, won't you?" Logan said.

Chapter 57

"Mr. March, can you hear me?"

The Gravedigger's voice from outside the cave, a harsh whisper from the darkness.

"I can hear you."

"We have to talk."

"We've got nothing to talk about."

"Gold. We can talk about gold."

March let a smile color his voice. "The time for that is way past."

"I've been so wrong, Mr. March. I've been wrong about everything."

March took the five rounds from his shirt pocket that old Benny Hinton had given him. He didn't believe bullets marked with a cross were needed to kill the Gravedigger. But it was better to be sure than sorry. He reloaded his Colt and waited . . .

In pain.

As far as March could tell, a bullet had entered the small of his back and was still inside him. His chest hurt and if he took a deep breath he tasted blood in his mouth.

It was a killing wound. He'd seen enough dying men to know that.

"Mr. March . . ."

"Yeah?"

"I've sent Logan and his men away from the cave. We must talk. We can work this out and become rich in the process."

"I don't trust you, Gravedigger."

March readied his gun.

I'm gonna kill you, Gravedigger. How about them beans?

"I have no weapon, Mr. March."

"Then step inside with your arms wide. Let me see you plain. It's as black as a steer's tongue in here."

"Will you shoot me?"

"I'll hold my fire."

"We can work it out, Mr. March."

"Yeah, I know we can."

A pause, then, "I'm coming in, Mr. March."

March carefully thumbed back the Colt's hammer, silently cussing ol' Sam's triple click.

"I'm inside, Mr. March."

March was startled. The cave was dark, the night was dark and the Gravedigger wore dark clothes. He couldn't see the man.

"Where the hell are you?" March said.

"Very close, Mr. March."

"Where, damn you?"

The rotten smell of decay filled March's nostrils, the stink of a dead hog that's lain in the sun for three days.

The Gravedigger's breath.

March brought up his Colt, but it snagged on the man's coat. Fingers closed around his throat.

Tightened.

"Die, Mr. March . . . die . . . and be damned. . . ."

March pulled the trigger.

The blast and flash of the gun in the narrow confines of the cave was like a lightning strike.

The Gravedigger shrieked, a high, piercing screech repeated over and over.

March heard his peg leg pound on the sand of the cave floor. He thumbed off a second shot, firing into darkness.

But the Gravedigger was gone.

Screams echoed through the night, one after another, like a woman screeching, growing distant. The man was running headlong, heedless of the dark cartwheeling around him.

Bullets whined and spat into the cave. March took cover behind rock until the fire ended.

He could no longer hear the Gravedigger.

He shook his head. "Where the hell did I hit him? A carved-up bullet right in the balls?" March pursed his lips. "Hell, that had to sting."

Chapter 58

Booker and the others heard the shot as they were entering the valley.

Logan threw an order over his shoulder, told everyone to halt, then galloped toward the cave.

The gunmen guarding the prisoners exchanged glances.

"Ol' Rance March made his break, you reckon?" one of them said.

"Seems like, or the Gravedigger shot him," another answered.

"Nah, he'd bury him first, then shoot him."

The men laughed, but their bellows were cut short as a skeletal figure bounded out of the darkness toward them, shrieking with every leap.

"He shot me," the Gravedigger screamed. Then, as though the full horror of the outrage had just dawned on him, "Me! He shot me!"

"You git him, Gravedigger?" This from a tall gunman with the hollowed-out face of a man who'd had a hungry childhood.

"Look at my arm," the Gravedigger screeched. "He near shot it clean off."

"Let me take a look," the lanky man said. Then he said again, "Did you gun the son of a bitch?"

The Gravedigger threw back his head and let out with a banshee wail. "He lives! He breathes! He's alive!"

"Well, don't that beat all?" the lanky man said.

"They say ol' Rance is a hard man to kill," a gunman said.

"Seems like." Lanky waved to the Gravedigger. "Let me see that arm. I'll tell you if'n you're done fer."

The Gravedigger held out his arm. His face was the color of death, his teeth bared in a grimace.

"Hell, take your coat off."

The Gravedigger did as he was told. The front of his white shirt was stained with blood.

Not his, but the blood of others.

The lanky man studied the arm, made the Gravedigger yelp a time or two, then said,"Bone's shattered above the elbow." His hooded gaze bridged the darkness. "It's gonna have to come off, to save your life, like. If it don't, the arm will rot an' so will you."

"I will not be maimed again!" the Gravedigger shrieked. "I can't inherit my destiny as a half man!"

Lanky shrugged. "Suit yourself."

One of the other gunmen laughed.

Booker, frightened by madness, tried to fade into the darkness. A man that crazy was unpredictable.

"Where is Logan?" the Gravedigger said, a man treading the ragged edge of hysteria.

"I guess he rode on to the cave," the lanky gunman said.

The Gravedigger turned, limping into the darkness, his words falling behind him.

"Kill him! Kill him, Logan! Let him feel what it's like."

The voice faded, and a man said,"What the hell? Do we stay out here all night?"

"Nah," the lanky man said. "We'll head to the cave. I could use some coffee."

"After your coffee, you gonna shoot March, Bob?" somebody asked.

"Why don't you do it yourself, Clem?" the lanky man said.

"Because I don't want to die."

"Neither do I."

"Then who goes into the cave and guns him?"

"Hell, I don't care, so long as it ain't me," the lanky man said.

Chapter 59

Cass Logan stood just to the right of the cave entrance.

"Rance, you awake?"

"Sure I'm awake. Visit from your pard the Grave-digger ruined my beauty sleep."

"You kill him?"

"Winged him or shot him in the balls. I can't make up my mind which."

"Maybe you shot his pecker off."

"Maybe."

"Rance, we need to sign a peace treaty."

"What are you offering, Cass?"

"Come out of the cave now and you and your hired hand can walk free."

"What about Booker and Mrs. Rowantree and her kid?"

"Them too."

"And if I don't?"

"Then I'll gun all of them and starve you out, Rance. You know I'll do it."

March was quiet for a while.

This dying business was easier than he thought, kind of like walking from one room into another. And there wasn't much pain and that surprised him. The bullet was deep, and it should bring discomfort to a man.

"Rance, you asleep in there?"

"No, I'm awake. I'm thinking hard about your proposition, Cass."

"Just don't think too long an' give yourself a headache. I'm not a patient man."

"What's the all-fired hurry, Cass? I got no food or water and you can wait until I turn up my toes."

Now there was a silence from Logan.

Finally he said, "A couple of my boys seen army patrols in the hills. I don't want them snooping around here, making trouble."

"Well, uh-huh, that's part of the reason, Cass."

"Damn you, Rance."

"What's the rest of it?"

"You know the rest of it," Logan said. "You heard the Gravedigger. There's gold and silver coin still in the cave."

"Just wanted to hear you say it, Cass." March grinned. "On account of how I found the gold. It's buried shallow, in iron chests, but I only uncovered one of them."

Logan couldn't keep the excitement out of his voice. "What was in it? Damn your eyes, Rance, tell me."

"Aw, I don't want to do that, getting you all worked up over nothing. The army's just gonna take it away from you, to buy cannons and the like."

"All right, Rance, you're in for a cut."

"How big?"

"Hell, an equal share, honest and true. Now what's in the damned chest?"

"Well, it's dark in here, but, near as I can figure, it's full of gold coins right enough." March grinned and decided to embroider his lie. "Found something else, an iron helmet and chest armor worn by one o' them old Spanish men."

"I want that gold, Rance," Logan said. "And you'll get your due, lay to that."

"I'll study on it, Cass. Come sunup I'll give you my answer."

"Rance, in the meantime, don't do nothing foolish. I mean, nothing with dynamite and that."

March was surprised. So there was dynamite in the cave.

A germ of an idea began to form in his brain.

"I found the dynamite, Cass," he lied again, "but I won't use it unless I have to. Hell, it could bring down the whole mountain."

"Just be careful with that stuff, Rance. It's old and sweaty—"

"Like me," March said.

"Yeah, well, be careful is all. I'll talk to you again at first light."

"Looking forward to it, Cass," March said.

March was sure his effort to find the dynamite would kill him. And it almost did.

By the time he found the box of explosives and returned to his hiding place, his wounds had reopened and he was covered with blood.

His head was light, spinning, and in the shadows he saw dead people, men and woman he'd known and a few he'd killed.

He forced himself to stay awake, moving now and then, welcoming the pain. If he slept, he'd die, and he wasn't ready for that.

Not yet.

March laid the dynamite beside him and, heedless of the danger, built and lit a smoke.

He waited for the dawn.

The pallid dead crowded close and whispered.

Chapter 60

Booker and the others were ordered to sit among the trees, away from the fire. Two gunmen with rifles stood guard.

Logan took delight in telling the prisoners they were now expendable.

"Ol' Rance don't give a shit about any of you, wants to dicker for the gold he found in the cave," he said. "Puts you in a bad position, don't it?"

"Let the woman and child go, Logan," Booker said.

The sheriff shook his head. "Hell no, I'm getting used to having you folks around."

He looked at Lafe. "All except you. Get on your feet."

But it was Booker who jumped up. "Leave that man alone," he said. "He works for Mr. March."

Lafe rose. "Archibald, you set back down," he said. "No point in you getting killed on my account."

Logan grinned. "You know what's in store for you, huh, black boy?"

"From white trash like you, Logan? Yeah, I know."

"You killed two of my men, and there's a third lying over there by the fire gut-shot. He won't last until dawn."

Lafe said nothing, and Logan said,"Now, if you ain't an uppity black boy, what are you?"

"A man with a killing hate in him, Logan. Just like you."

Logan nodded. "Right you are. Only it's me that's gonna do the killing." He turned to one of the riflemen. "Get a rope and find a high cottonwood."

The man smiled. "Anything you say, Cass."

It took Lafe Stringfellow more than ten minutes to die. He strangled slowly, legs kicking, eyes popping, tongue lolling out of his head.

Thinking back on it later, Booker recalled that there was tragedy in Lafe's death, but no dignity.

But he'd met his end like a man, showing no fear to his enemies, and that was a good thing to remember him by.

After it was done, Logan looked up at the swaying body, the rope creaking in the silence of the night.

Booker searched the man's face, looking for a sign of remorse. There was none. The sheriff was smiling.

"Boys, that's the first black I've hung since I left Texas," he said.

A man laughed. "Feel good, Cass?"

"Damn right it feels good. Hanging a man is better than poking a woman, any day of the week."

He looked around at his assembled gunman, grinning. "But it gives a man an appetite. What's in the grease for supper?"

Logan was eating when the Gravedigger hobbled from the darkness, frantically, like a headless chicken.

When he saw the sheriff he renewed his shrill shrieks.

"He shot me," the Gravedigger screamed. "He hit my arm."

Logan sat where he was, a forkful of bacon and beans suspended between his mouth and plate. In the distance thunder grumbled and the sky flashed.

"What the hell do you want me to do about it?" Logan said.

"Kill him!"

Logan went back to his grub. "Kill him your own self."

"Look at my arm, Mr. Logan," the Gravedigger said. His voice was now a pathetic whine.

"I see it."

"One of the men told me it needs to be cut off."

"Seems like. If you don't, it'll rot."

"I can't be maimed. I must come into my inheritance whole."

"You ain't whole to begin with. You got a wooden leg, remember?"

Logan grinned. "Anyhow, nobody here is gonna cut the damned thing off, so don't worry about it."

"Clean my wound, Mr. Logan. Bind it up."

"Get the woman to do it."

"She'll hurt me."

"So will I."

Logan's fork scraped on the tin plate as he rounded up the last, greasy scraps of food.

Then he looked up at the Gravedigger. "I don't need you anymore, you crazy old fool. Now git out of here."

The Gravedigger looked horrified. "But . . . but the gold."

"March found it. I'm dickering with him."

"But there is no—" The man stopped, knowing he'd gone four words too far.

"What did you say?" Logan asked.

The Gravedigger backtracked. "I mean, March is lying. Only I know where the gold is hidden. He didn't find it."

"Well, now, he says he did. Gold coins in iron chests."

"He's lying, Mr. Logan."

"I don't think so."

Logan got to his feet. "You're leaving, Gravedigger. Get your hoss, then ride away and die when that arm rots and falls off'n you."

The Gravedigger jumped up and down, screeching again. He looked around him.

"Men, those of you who are loyal, flock to my side," he called out.

No one moved and a couple of men sniggered.

"You loco old coot, you're done," Logan said. "Now get out of here or you'll hang beside the black boy."

Lightning flashes threw the cavernous hollows of the Gravedigger's face into shadows that came and went.

"Logan," he said, "you'll regret this."

The sheriff smiled. "You don't scare me none, old man. Now git or I'll change my mind and gun you."

The Gravedigger turned away, then stopped. He looked at Logan. "Give me the woman and child."

"What fer? You thinking on getting a little ass, maybe?"

"I want to bury them. When I raise them up, they'll be my handmaidens." His voice took on a pleading tone. "Logan, I also crave nourishment."

The sheriff grinned and shook his head. "Then you're out of luck, crazy man. I reckon I'll want the woman later, maybe tonight. Wait. . . ."

He looked over to where the prisoners were sitting. "Take Archibald."

"A poor substitute."

"Well, it's him or nothing. I'll hog-tie him for you and put him on a hoss."

"Then he'll have to do," the Gravedigger said. "If nothing else, he'll nourish me."

Thunder crashed and lightning flared. Booker felt a sense of dread as Logan, a grin on his face from ear to ear, came at him with a rope.

The madman was by the fire, framed by shimmering scarlet, as though standing amid the fires of hell.

Chapter 61

Booker's hands were tied behind his back, his mouth gagged with a rag, as the Gravedigger led his horse out of the valley.

The madman had a shotgun in a boot under his left knee, a Colt in his waistband, a shovel tied to his saddle.

Lightning scrawled across the sky like the signature of a tyrant signing a death warrant. Thunder bullied and threatened and the wind fled through the woods, bending the pines in its haste. There was no rain yet, but the damp air smelled dank, of green moss and black earth.

Booker bowed his head, determined to be brave.

But he was as scared as a child staring into a dark closet.

The Gravedigger slowed his horse and let Booker come alongside. The man's face swam out of the darkness, as white and sinister as a *Dia de los Muertos* sugar skull.

"Your ordeal will end soon, my friend," the Gravedigger said, his voice raised against the racket of the storm. "Your day of reckoning has been delayed too long."

Because of the gag, Booker was unable to speak, but he was certain his eyes telegraphed fear.

Lightning flashes glistened wetly on the Gravedigger's left arm, the shattered limb still seeping blood.

"It is a great honor," he said.

The Gravedigger turned his face to the torn sky.

"Behold, Mr. Booker, even the gods rejoice in the justness of my cause. After I lay you to rest, I will deal with the traitor Logan and his minions. As you lie in the grave you will know that your life's blood surges in my veins and sustains me as I undertake that task. How you will laugh at Logan's undoing."

The madman turned and his gaze sought Booker's face.

"I can see in your eyes how excited you are, and that is good," he said. He smiled. "Patience, Mr. Booker. Not long now."

By the time they clattered onto the hardpan, thunder and lightning ripped the night apart and sheets of rain whipped in the wind.

The Gravedigger headed directly for the arroyo where Booker had sheltered with Mrs. Rowantree and her daughter.

Booker knew the man had never been there before. It seemed that he was guided by instinct, like a predatory animal.

Under his torn shirt, it looked to Booker as though his chest had been slashed to the bone by the Gravedigger's talons.

Angry red welts, all of them beaded with dewdrops of blood, ran from his right shoulder almost to his left side. The wounds burned, as though he'd been splashed by acid.

The Gravedigger's good humor had vanished once they'd entered the arroyo clearing. He'd reached up and dragged Booker from his horse, his long fingernails raking like the tines of a pitchfork.

The man's strength was enormous, and Booker, his hands tied, could not resist as he'd been dragged under a tree and dumped hard on the ground.

"I will dine soon," he said, staring down at Booker. "You will wait for me."

Now Booker watched the Gravedigger.

The man's shadowy figure was already thigh-deep in a muddy grave. Lightning flashes glinted on the blade of the shovel he wielded.

He used only his right arm to dig and paused often. He leaned against the side of the grave as though exhausted, then started again.

Rain rattled through the leaves of the tree and ticked on the ground.

Booker looked around him.

The Gravedigger's horse stood, head down, about twenty yards away. The shotgun was still in the boot, but the man had his Colt in his waistband.

As thunder rumbled, Booker began to work his hands, trying to create some stretch in the rope.

Within a couple of minutes, the knot loosened easily. Too easily . . .

He'd benefited from another of Cass Logan's little jokes.

Chapter 62

Booker freed his hands, but kept them behind his back.

The Gravedigger hadn't checked his bonds, trusting that Logan had done a good job.

It had been a bad mistake.

The sheriff had tied Booker's wrists with some kind of slipknot that let the rope slide through easily.

Giving Booker a sporting chance to escape had been not been part of Logan's motive. He'd wanted only to play a joke on the Gravedigger—and he'd succeeded.

Booker watched the Gravedigger intently.

The man was suffering from a massive loss of blood and his motions were slowing. Given time, his shattered arm would kill him. But Booker could not wait that long.

The Gravedigger could still shoot him, wound him, then drag him alive and kicking to the grave he'd dug.

Booker shuddered as fear clutched at him.

He had to . . . What was it March had called it? Make his play.

Slowly, never taking his eyes off the madman, he got

his feet under him. The night was dark, but the lightning flashes were coming fast, little time between them.

He'd rely on the thunder.

He waited. A roaring boom. Booker counted off seconds. Then stopped when the lightning shimmered, illuminating the clearing in stark white.

He'd count again. Make sure. Thunder banged, then . . . one, Mississippi . . . two, Mississippi . . . three, Mississippi . . .

A flash.

Three seconds to reach the scattergun on the Gravedigger's horse.

Maybe less.

And then what? Engage the man in a gunfight he was sure to lose?

Booker tilted back his head, opened his dry-as-a-stick mouth to rainwater.

He'd cross that bridge when he came to it.

Thunder slammed, echoed around the clearing.

And Booker was up and running.

Made nervous by the storm, the Gravedigger's horse shied away from him, arcs of white showing in its eyes.

Lightning flashed and Booker dived his full length onto the grass.

The Gravedigger was still working. He hadn't looked around, intent on his task.

Booker rose and tried again, lunging for the shotgun. This time the horse trotted away from him, rapidly putting distance between them.

Cursing under his breath, Booker gave up on the Greener.

The Gravedigger had his back to him and was now almost waist-deep in the hole he'd dug.

The man was screaming, raving, asking one question over and over again, "What's it like? What's it like?"

Rain pounding on him, Booker now used the lightning. It did not fail him, pointing the way to a jumbled pile of rocks a few yards way.

He chose a boulder about the size of a ripe watermelon.

And walked slowly, carefully, toward the grave, the *swish, swish* of his feet through the long grass lost in the bellowing bedlam of the storm.

The Gravedigger turned at the last second, saw Booker, and his eyes got big. He tried to protect himself with the shovel, swinging it up to guard his head.

Too late.

The boulder, swung with all of Booker's strength, smashed into the top of the man's head. The Gravedigger screeched and fell on his back.

Booker went after him. He jumped on top of the man's body. He bent, grabbed the shovel, and threw it away from him. He took the Colt from the man's waistband, shoved it in his own, then, with an agility born of fear and revulsion, scrambled out of the muddy hole.

Outlined by lightning bursts, Booker stood at the edge of the grave and looked down at the writhing man at the bottom.

The rain fell heavier, in torrents.

"Help me!" the Gravedigger screamed, blood mixed with water streaming down his face. "Get me out of here."

He screamed louder when the first shovelful of dirt fell on top of him.

Chapter 63

It was easy to die. Not so easy to stay alive.

Ransom March fought death, aware of its sleepy seduction. So easy, so fine, so pleasurable, like rolling on top of a beautiful woman, her body perfumed and warm, thighs open, welcoming.

Good for a man.

Big ol' Bill Wilkie knew March was dying. He stood in the shadows and watched, his face unmoving.

Then he said,"Let it go, Rance. Your time is done."

March smiled. "Still sore at me, Bill, huh?"

"There was no call for you to do it that way, Rance. My wife and kids were right there."

"I couldn't take a chance on you, Bill. Is how it was."

"The cabin was my home, Rance. My wife and family were right there. In my home."

"I figured maybe you were heeled. You could have had a hideout."

"I was standing in my drawers, just out of bed. You knowed I didn't have no hideout."

"Ah, them was hard times right enough, Bill. A man had no time to think, just do."

"A shotgun, Rance. You cut me in half. My wife and kids were splashed with guts and shit."

"You robbed the banks, Bill. And the trains. An' you killed a lawman."

"I know, but you didn't need to do it when my wife and kids were right there."

"Thinking back on it, I could have done it different. I'm sorry, Bill."

"Sorry don't cut it, Rance."

March watched good ol' Bill Wilkie for a while, until the man faded into the rock wall of the cave.

He shook his head. Bill was right. A ten-gauge Greener loaded with buck makes a mess of a man. Especially when his wife and kids are right there.

He looked at the mouth of the cave. The rain was coming down hard, in torrents.

He built a cigarette, hoping the dead would not pay another visit. It was a chore for a man to justify something he'd done twenty years before, when he was younger and his blood was up.

Hell, Bill should have known that.

March was about to light his cigarette, but hesitated. He counted the matches in his pocket. Three, more than enough for what he had to do.

He lit his smoke, trying to figure. Four hours until sunup, maybe less. He had to hold on that long. Thank God he had no pain. If he'd been gut-shot, he probably would've killed himself before this.

That was lucky.

Lightning turned the raindrops falling outside the cave into steel needles, and an errant wind scattered his cigarette smoke.

March wondered if Lester was still alive.

The man was mouthy and Cass Logan would only take so much.

The Gravedigger was mad and unpredictable and he might already have done for him.

Lester had been raised as a gentleman, a quality that didn't guarantee survival in the New Mexico Territory.

Too bad, he was a nice kid.

Chapter 64

"Please, not the grave!"

The Gravedigger tried to rise, but the blow to his head had done something to his legs and he couldn't move.

Booker threw in another shovelful of dirt.

"I'll give you anything, Mr. Booker," the man screamed. "Wealth, power, beautiful women, anything you want."

"I want you dead," Booker said.

"I can't die," the Gravedigger said. "I will lie here forever with the scarlet worms."

"You did it to others," Booker said. "Now shut the hell up and take a dose of your own medicine."

The man was beyond coherent speech. With every shovel of muddy dirt that fell on him, he grew more terror-stricken and shrieked louder.

Finally, his eyes popping out of his head, he managed "What's it like?"

"I don't give a damn," Booker said.

"What's it—"

Dirt fell on his face, into his mouth. The Grave-digger's clawed hands reached up through the mud, a supplicant pleading for life to a heedless execu-tioner.

More dirt fell on him.

His pleas stopped.

Then his shrieks.

Then silence.

Booker kept shoveling until the hole was filled.

He threw the shovel down and sat on the grave, the mud pockmarked by tiny pools of rain.

The Gravedigger had cheated the worms once, but Booker was determined he would not do it a second time. If the ground heaved under him, he'd throw on more dirt and more. He'd move a mountain if neces-sary.

"Abide right where you are," Booker said aloud. "And stay dead this time, you son of a bitch."

The long night had ended, the dawn came and went, and Booker continued to sit on the grave.

Once, in the darkness, the coyotes had come close and their cries had scraped his nerves raw. He'd seen them, moving like gray ghosts, smelling the dead.

The grave was still, churned by the falling rain, and had turned to liquid mud.

Chilled, soaked to the skin, Booker finally got to his feet.

The Gravedigger was now as dead as he was ever

going to be. The rock had paralyzed his legs, and four feet of muddy dirt had finished him off.

Booker felt no remorse. As March would say, the man needed killing.

But he knew he'd been lucky.

The Gravedigger had turned his back on him, so he'd gotten the drop.

Now he knew what March had been talking about. Getting the drop on a man was much to be desired.

It was a matter of survival. Him or me.

He'd judged March too harshly, Booker realized. He had condemned the man for something he'd now done himself.

He'd gotten the drop and gladly taken advantage of it.

If he'd managed to reach the scattergun, he would have shot the Gravedigger in the back, with not a second thought about the right or the wrong of the thing.

Booker glanced at the sky, the clouds like sheets of curled lead.

It dawned on him then that there had never been a Prince of the Plains, just hard men doing their best to survive in a hard land, often with every man's hand turned against them.

Rance March had been such a man and, as a peace officer, he'd done what he had to do, any way he could.

He'd lived this long because he'd always sought the drop on bad men. Cutting a man in half with a shotgun as he bounced a baby on his knee or while his head was bowed in prayer was a hard, harsh thing.

But it had to be done.

City fathers didn't hire saints as town marshals. They wanted killers who knew how to get the drop on a man.

Men like March.

And, Booker thought, *men like myself.*

He was learning.

Chapter 65

"Rance?"

March had been asleep. He opened his eyes, mildly surprised that he was still alive.

"What do you want, Cass?"

"Brung you coffee."

"Bring it in. Take two steps into the cave, lay the cup down, then get the hell out."

"Anything you say, Rance."

Logan did as he'd been told, but on his way back, he hesitated at the cave opening. Rain lashed down behind him.

"You think it over, Rance?"

"I can drill ya from here."

"I'm not wearing my gun, Rance. Plain to see."

After a moment, March said,"Yeah, I thought it over. I'm in. For a double share."

"That's niggardly, Rance, mighty cold."

"You heard me."

Logan smiled. "Hell, all right, you can have the Gravedigger's share. He ain't coming back."

He shoved out his hand, caught rainwater in his cupped palm, then drank. When he was finished, he wiped his mouth and said,"I used the woman this morning. Gives a man a thirst."

"Get the hell out and let me drink my coffee," March said.

"When do I get the gold?"

"After I drink my coffee."

"Tell me again, Rance. How much gold there?"

"Enough for everybody. Bring the boys with you, all of them. Gold is heavy."

"Sure thing, Rance." Logan smiled. "Well, I'll leave you to your coffee. Just holler when you're ready."

"Remember, I want all the boys in here, to keep an eye on them, like."

"Hell, just try keeping them rannies out, Rance." Logan grinned.

March drank coffee and smoked the last of his tobacco. He'd roll his next cigarette in hell.

He'd never been on speaking terms with God, and to ask for His mercy now when he'd never asked it before didn't set well with him. Probably wouldn't set well with God either.

He looked into the shadows. Ol' Bill Wilkie was gone. March smiled. He couldn't believe that Bill was still mad at him after all these years.

Getting cut in half with a scattergun altered a man's thinking, made him downright testy.

Well, he and Bill would talk it over soon, put the bad feelings to rest.

March drained the coffee cup and struggled to his feet. The pain had returned, as though somebody had driven a red-hot bayonet through him from back to front.

His time was short, he knew.

He staggered to the front of the cave, breathing hard, holding on to a wall for support, and looked outside, into the rain-swept morning.

He saw Lafe.

The bastards had hung him.

When?

March tried to think. It must have happened while he'd been asleep in the cave. He'd heard nothing because Lafe Stringfellow was not a man to beg for his life and holler at the approach of death.

A sadness in him that was worse than the pain of his wound, March looked for a long time at Lafe's body as it swayed with the whims of the wind.

He'd been a good man, ol' Lafe, and a top hand. He knew cows and horses and the range and, for the most part, stayed clear of white women and ardent spirits.

March's epitaph for Lafe was not much as they go, but the man would have understood and agreed with every word.

Lafe had died, and now Cass Logan needed killing.

It meant a slight change of plan, but killing Logan was a thing that had to be done.

He'd given March no choice in the matter.

Chapter 66

March retreated into the cave. He stuck a stick of dynamite into his waistband, then braced his back against a wall, his Colt against his leg.

"Cass Logan!" he yelled. "Bring the boys and let's dig fer gold."

A pause, then, "Is that you, Rance?"

"Yeah. Didn't you hear me?"

"Nah, damned rain's too loud."

"Well, I said bring the boys and we'll dig for gold."

"Be right there, Rance."

A minute passed, then another; then finally Logan and his men trooped into the cave, a few carrying shovels.

Well, now . . .

Maybe the reason was that Rance March was sick, slowed down by his wound. Maybe he hesitated just a moment to get a clear shot at Logan.

Maybe there was no reason.

How could he have anticipated that Logan would step into the cave, raise his gun, and shoot him?

Some things a man can guard against, but March

had not considered that possibility and he'd left himself wide-open.

He hit the ground and from far off heard Logan laugh and say, "Enjoy your share, old man. No gold, just lead."

Men laughed with him. Then their laughter receded as they walked deeper into the cave.

March was hit hard, a well-placed shot to the middle of his chest.

He figured the bullet had burst his heart asunder, and that it wouldn't pump much longer.

How long did he have? Seconds if he was lucky.

He crawled toward the cave entrance. He heard Logan's men curse, rage and frustration spewing out of them like pus from a lanced boil.

March grinned. Now they knew there were no gold coins.

Cuss away, boys. You can't kill me twice.

A yard from the cave mouth . . .

He thumbed a match into flame and lit the dynamite fuse. The fuse smoked and sputtered and started to burn down fast.

"Dynamite!" a man yelled. It sounded like Logan.

Feet pounded, frightened men fighting to get out of what had now become a death trap . . . and a grave.

"Yeeehah!" March yelled, grinning, his eyes fixed on the dynamite stick in his hands. "How does this set—"

Boom!

The explosion killed March without pain.

The mountain didn't fall, but a chunk of it did.

Boulders, some as big as hayricks, rained down, piling up at the cave entrance.

The men trapped inside saw three feet of light at the top of the rock pile . . . then two . . . then a foot . . . then nothing.

The cave plunged into darkness.

Men, smashed and maimed when part of the roof fell, screamed in mortal agony. The unhurt screeched in fear. The dead made no sound at all.

They were the lucky ones.

Chapter 67

Lester Booker stepped away from the grave and moved to the wall of the arroyo. The pounding rain found him and he moved again, to a place just as wet.

He was wishful for coffee, but had none. He stopped thinking about it.

Because of lightning and leaden light, his eyes played tricks on him. He was sure the grave was seething, bubbling upward like muddy coffee boiling over in a pot.

But when he drew the Colt from his waistband and walked through the downpour to investigate, he saw only the play of rain on mud, and a hundred small puddles shimmering in the lightning flashes.

By now the Gravedigger was dead.

Had to be.

Booker walked back to the wall and waited.

For what he did not know.

The morning wore on, dark, gloomy, dragging its feet, refusing to shade into a sullen afternoon.

Every now and then Booker checked the grave, not out of idle curiosity, but fear.

He was returning to the wall when he heard the blast of an explosion followed by a rumble that sounded like apples tumbling into a wooden barrel.

Later, Booker could not recall if he knew right then that it was all over.

That Rance March was dead and the reckoning had come.

But he was sure he did.

A woman would call it intuition. A man instinct. Either way, it was a . . . knowing.

There was no accounting for the ways of a horse.

This time the Gravedigger's mount stood quietly and Booker swung into the saddle. He tipped his plug hat over his eyes, left the arroyo, and rode onto the storm-thrashed hardpan.

The wind had quit fooling around and now squalled with considerable force, tossing the trees, driving the rain before it.

Lightning lit up the dark draws between the clouds and thunder rolled through them, bellowing like a stampeding herd.

Booker, aware that he was the tallest lightning target on the hardpan, urged his horse into a fast trot, then a canter.

He rode into the valley, drew rein, then scanned the ground ahead of him. Nothing moved but the wind, and the only sound was the fall of the rain.

It looked as though the explosion he'd heard had killed everybody.

Booker was a pilgrim, but he was smart. He'd learned

from March that a man doesn't charge headlong into danger. He bides his time, chooses his position, and lets the danger come to him.

He stepped out of the saddle and led his horse into the trees. He slid the shotgun from the boot, then adjusted the position of his Colt.

Now he waited. And watched.

Fat raindrops dropped through the tree canopy and thudded onto his hat. The day smelled of wet grass and muddy earth.

Ten minutes passed and Booker grew restless.

Then he saw the man.

A tall man wearing a slicker led two horses out of a patch of piñon and wild oak. One of the animals was saddled; the other was a packhorse, burdened with two canvas panniers.

As Booker watched, the man disappeared behind the trees that stood outside the cave.

There could be only one reason for the packhorse—he was about to load up the Spanish gold.

Chapter 68

At first thought, Booker figured he'd let the man ride out without interference. He had no interest in the treasure, and it was probably cursed anyhow.

Then he thought it through and changed his mind.

What if Rance was still alive? A share of the gold surely belonged to him.

And Mrs. Rowantree. After what she'd gone through, she deserved a share.

Booker decided he'd talk nice to the man, whoever he was, and show him the error of his ways. Gentleman to gentleman, without violence. The way it should be in these modern times of 1890.

But he didn't leave the scattergun behind when he stepped out of the trees and walked across the open ground to the cave.

Rance March had also taught him to be careful.

When Booker rounded the trees and saw the cave, he stopped in his tracks.

The man loading the gold watched him come, dismissed him, and went back to his task. Over his shoulder, he said, "They're all dead."

"Rance March?"

"Dead with the rest of them."

"Mrs. Rowantree?"

"The whore?"

Booker decided it was easier to nod.

"She's around, somewhere. And the kid."

"A share of the gold belongs to her."

Now the man turned. He had a lantern-jawed face, a huge Texas mustache, and cold eyes that had seen things.

"Well, she ain't gettin' any, Archibald. On account of how I need it all fer my own self."

"How come you survived?" Booker said, putting a heavy emphasis on the "you."

The gunman bent, picked up a gold plate, and dropped it into a pannier. "Call of nature, Archibald. Lucky for me, unlucky for them inside as is missing my company."

"Logan?"

The man shrugged. "In the damned cave. By this time, if he ain't dead, he's wishing he was. Take a regiment a week to clear them rocks away."

"And Rance March is in there?"

"I'm guessing the old coot brought the mountain down." The gunman smiled. "He was a mean one, ol' Rance."

The last of the gold was loaded.

"Well, Archibald, nice talking to you, but I got to be on my way."

"The name's Lester. And you're leaving half the gold here."

The man's smile slipped. "You know who you're talking to, Archibald? I go by Dave Battles. Name mean anything to you?"

The gunman pulled his slicker back from his holstered Colt.

"Not a damned thing," Booker said.

"It should. I'm a named man south of the Red."

"You may be, but I'm holding a named shotgun, goes by Greener."

"Ever shoot a man, Archibald?"

"There's a first time for everything."

"Thought so. You don't have the belly for it."

Battles drew, very fast and slick.

Booker squeezed the triggers of the scattergun.

Blasted in the belly by both barrels at a range of eight feet, Battles exploded, dead when what was left of him hit the ground.

"The name," Booker said, looking down at the man, "is Lester."

Chapter 69

Booker found a sheltered spot among the trees and dry wood enough to start a fire. Using Battles's supplies, he put coffee on to boil and sliced bacon into a pan.

The bacon was sizzling, turning brown, when Eliza Rowantree and Judith stepped through the trees.

Booker watched them come.

At a distance, Eliza still looked pretty, almost beautiful in the misty light, her torn dress enhancing her wide-hipped, large-breasted figure.

She should have stayed at a distance.

Up close, her face showed a network of lines, especially around the mouth and the corners of her eyes. Some of them makeup would cover; the rest were permanent life scars that would remain.

"Smelled your coffee and bacon," she said.

She sat on the damp grass by the fire, Judith, as always, her shadow.

"Tell me," she said.

"The Gravedigger is dead," Booker said. "Dead and buried."

"You killed him?"

"Yes. I got the drop on him."

"You shot him?" Eliza sounded incredulous.

"Hit him with a rock, then buried him."

"Alive?"

Booker smiled. "It was how he'd have wanted it."

The woman shuddered, then, "Will he stay buried?"

"He has so far. I think."

"Rance is dead." She nodded to the cave. "Behind that."

"I know."

Booker fried bread in the bacon grease and made sandwiches for all of them.

Talking around a mouthful of food, he said,"I killed a man over there."

"I heard the shot," Eliza said.

"Said his name was Dave Battles."

"I remember him. He hurt me bad."

"Well, he won't hurt you again," Booker said. "R-I-P a Texas gunfighter who reckoned he was faster than the triggers on a scattergun."

Eliza said nothing, and Booker stepped into the silence.

"He was trying to take the gold. I offered him half, but he wanted it all."

"You taking it back to New York?" Eliza said.

Booker shook his head. "The gold is for you and Judith. God knows, you both deserve it."

"We don't want it, Lester. Me and Judith will get by."

Booker was stunned. "But, Mrs. Rowantree, it's worth thousands."

"It's covered in blood, Lester. Selling sacred things that have been desecrated will bring nothing but bad luck. Everybody who ever wanted the treasure died horribly, including Ransom March."

She took a bite out of her sandwich. "I want nothing to do with it."

"But . . . but you and Judith could start a new life, you—"

"I told you, we'll get by. I can find work in Santa Fe."

"What will I do with it?"

"Bury it deep, Lester. Bury it where it will never be found."

After he parted from Eliza and Judith, Booker loaded the gold onto the packhorse.

He crossed the hardpan and rode into the arroyo.

He found the shovel, then brought the packhorse to the grave. A coyote had shit on the packed dirt, and that pleased Booker immensely.

When he dug into the grave, he smelled the Grave-digger's body. The man was already beginning to rot.

"You planned to resurrect all those people you buried," Booker said, "but you couldn't resurrect yourself."

He dug down a couple of feet and tossed the Spanish treasure on top of the Gravedigger. Then he carefully covered up the hole so it looked as though it had never been.

Then he picked up the coyote shit on the shovel and replaced it.

* * *

Booker rode onto the hardpan and swung south toward Santa Fe.

The shotgun was under his knee, the Colt in his waistband.

The rain had stopped and the sky was clearing.

He smiled.

The first thing he was going to do when he got home—

No, wait—that was the second thing.

The first thing was to write the story of Ransom March, as he was, a brave man who had done his best and didn't always play by the rules.

Now, for the second thing . . .

He planned to throw Miss Lucy McIntyre, his betrothed, on a bed.

And have his wicked way with her.

The thrilling Trail Drive series returns!
Don't miss

THE AMARILLO TRAIL

A Ralph Compton Novel by Jory Sherman
coming from Signet in May 2011.

Doc smelled the burning hair and hide a few minutes before he rode up on the branding corral, some two miles from his ranch house. The odor floated on the stiff breeze that still scoured the arroyos, rippled the waters of the tanks, and made the grass sway and flow like an emerald ocean. The scent gave him a good feeling. He knew that the gather, which would increase the size of his herd, was almost over and his calves would soon all bear the brand of the Slash B ranch.

Tad Rankin, his foreman, raised a hand in greeting as Doc rode up. He pulled the branding iron away from the calf's left hip and stuck it back into the fire, resting the shaft on one of the stones in the fire ring. Two hands, Joadie Lee Bostwick and Curly Bob Naylor, released the branded calf and watched it wobble off to where two other hands shooed it through the partially open pole gate, where it cantered to its waiting mother, tail wagging like a puppy dog's.

"Ho, Doc," Rankin called out. "You been getting any younger since I saw you this mornin'?"

" 'Bout as much as you got smarter since sunup, Tad. Give up the brandin' for a second, will you?"

Tad spoke to another hand nearby and walked over to the rails and climbed through. His lean body gave him plenty of room. He took off his heavy gloves and slapped them against his leg before tucking them in an empty back pocket. He spat out a stream of tobacco juice and shifted the wad in his mouth to the other side.

Doc dismounted and looped his reins around a pole, then started walking some distance from the corral. Tad walked beside him, knowing the boss was going to give him orders or chew his ass out for something.

"You got something on your mind, Doc?" Rankin asked.

"I'm gettin' together a drive to Salina over in Kansas territory. But it's a little complicated."

"We ain't ready for no drive to Kansas right off, Doc. We're nigh to the end of the gather and I can't spare no men."

"Your men ain't a-goin', Tad."

"Pretty hard to make a drive thouten no drovers."

"I'm makin' two drives, Tad. I mean my sons are. Puttin' together three thousand head and five hundred of them will come from this herd. The biggest and the fattest."

"Oh, we can put five hundred head to pasture along the Canadian all right, and still have plenty to spare."

"We gotta move fast. I'm ridin' down to Dumas this evenin' to start Miles out and I want two hundred fifty head driven down there come mornin'. Need to put trail brands on them afore you set out."

"Jesus Christ," Tad said. "We're still puttin' the Slash B on calves, Doc. Now I got to stop and trail brand two hundred fifty perfectly contented cattle and move them all the way down to Miles's spread. Hell, why can't he pick 'em up on his way out to Kansas?"

"Because I don't want him or his brother to know I'm sending two herds on the drive east."

"You got good reason to do such a tomfool thing, I reckon."

"You know why, Tad."

Tad sucked in a deep breath that was like a penny-whistle the way it sounded. He nodded.

Both Jared and Miles had fallen for the same woman, Caroline Vickers. Back in high school. She had kept both boys guessing until they were all in their early twenties. Caroline was nineteen when she chose to marry Miles Blaine, who was twenty-one. Jared was twenty-three and thought he deserved to marry Caroline because he was the elder and had more land than either his father or Miles. He was furious and, before the wedding—which he had refused to attend—he beat up Miles. It was a brutal fight, and when Doc broke it up, Jared vowed that he would someday get Caroline away from his brother.

"How you goin' to do that?" Ethyl asked her son.

"I'm going to kill Miles and then Caroline will have to come to me."

"They'll throw you in prison, Jared. Maybe even hang you," Doc had said.

"Miles ain't gonna know what hit him and I sure as hell ain't goin' to tell. I won't be arrested for nothin' and I'll give the grievin' widder a home she can be proud of."

"You better not talk that way, Jared," his mother had said. "The Lord will strike you down if you even think about killin' your brother."

Yes, Rankin knew all about Caroline and how she had kept both boys guessing until the last minute when she had chosen to marry Miles. That choice puzzled everyone, just about, until people began to look back and compare the two boys. Miles was easygoing and so adoring of Caroline, she could dominate him. He responded to her every whim. Jared, however, was aggressive, bossy, and demanded, instead of asked, for everything he wanted. And he wanted Caroline to worship him and obey his every command. People saw these traits in all three at church, pie socials, and dances. Jared was the jealous one and Caroline kept him dangling until she was staring spinsterhood in the face and chose Miles to be her husband.

"Tad, I'll expect those two hundred fifty head in Dumas in two days."

"Three," Rankin said.

"Three, then, but I'll be back and you'd better have another two hundred fifty head ready for the trip to Jared's up in Perryton."

"I can do that, Doc."

"I'm off then. I expect you to carry out these tasks. As the contracts I signed said, 'time is of the essence.' I got to deliver three thousand head to Salina by June first. If we beat that deadline, the price goes up a dollar or two."

"This time of year, I don't know," Rankin said. "Them rivers can be powerfully brutal. You might lose a few head and you might lose some time. And, if them two boys meet up, you got a shit pile of trouble."

"Miles will start out first. He should get plenty of ground between him and Jared before Jared even leaves the barn."

"You hope."

"That's how I've got it figgered, Tad."

With that, Doc walked back to his horse with Tad and climbed into the saddle. He waved good-bye and rose off to the south toward Dumas.

He knew Miles would come through and get together a herd. Jared might be harder to convince. They had all made a cattle drive or two, one to Wyoming, another to Colorado. They hadn't made much money and lost quite a few head on both those drives.

It wasn't Miles he was worried about as he rode across his spread toward the main road between Amarillo and Dumas. It was Caroline. She wanted Miles under her thumb and she'd fight him all the way as she had in the past. When Miles was gone, she had no control over him and she was a jealous woman.

Buzzards flew in lazy circles in the sky. He knew what they were eyeing and sniffing out. A wolf had gotten one of the yearling calves a few days before and the scent of decomposing beef was still in the air. Nature held sway in the far reaches of his ranch and there was nothing he could do about it. In the past, he had fought off marauding Apaches, cattle rustlers, wolves, and mangy coyotes. The land wasn't the problem. It was ownership of the land that brought responsibility and guardianship. What he had must be protected. He looked on his ranch as a garden in olden times, like Eden. There were dangers lurking in every shadow, along every creek, and in every gully or arroyo. Men tended the land and its crops of hay and cattle, but he had to tend to his men. There were gray hairs for every challenge he had faced, every setback he had overcome.

As long as the easterners demanded beef, he would thrive, he knew. Next year, he could put together his own large herd and drive them to the railhead. That would pay off his mortgage so he and Ethyl could finally enjoy the fruits of their labors. Then his garden would become another Eden and he would be its god.

National Bestselling Author

RALPH COMPTON

S543-110310